First Encounter

He stood there, staring down at me with eyebrows raised. He was very male, that much I *did* notice even in my befuddled state. But he couldn't have been more than a year older than I. His hair was wavy, and very black, and his eyes were, too, like Mediterranean princes we've seen in Renaissance paintings. The look in those eyes made me feel like a specimen under a microscope. He wasn't very tall, not much taller than I, but he didn't seem small. He didn't seem like an athlete either. A panther, that was it — a black panther prepared to spring. Somebody who could be dangerous, something said inside my head. Only I wasn't frightened. I was far too angry.

point

THE GREAT RIP-OFF

Lavinia Harris

SCHOLASTIC INC.
New York Toronto London Auckland Sydney Tokyo

ISBN 0-590-33059-4

12 11 10 9 8 7 6 5 4 3 2 1   11   4 5 6 7 8 9/8

Printed in the U. S. A.   01

THE GREAT
RIP-OFF

Chapter 1

SSW Enterprises, Computer Consultants (Discretion Guaranteed); Sidney Scott Webster, President.

Who'd have thought I'd turn out to be a computer genius? Not to mention president of a company, doing hush-hush detective work, when I'm not quite sixteen? Certainly not me on the day it all began, the first Monday in February, the start of a new semester.

That Monday turned out to be, in more ways than one, a very surprising day, from the moment I first walked in Dad's office door. No, actually, my being in his hospital office in the middle of a school day had been the first surprise. It certainly had not been on the agenda. Dad at the breakfast table had been in what Mother called his "professional abstraction" (heaven forbid we should say he was "psyched out," which is what he calls it when it's me). Mother had her nose in a notebook and her eyes in an old cookbook she'd found somewhere, obviously debating whether to get on with that cookbook she's always threatening to write herself. I cut out as soon as I'd finished eating, because Cordelia Quinn was waiting on the corner for me to listen to the latest installment of the long-running soap opera between her and Steve Wiczniewski.

Cordelia's my best friend and practically a sister and I'd trust her with my life, but no way do I trust what she keeps threatening about breaking off with Steve. That's about as likely as my getting romantic about Ceegee. Steve's a senior and the star of Lakeland High School's basketball team, and Cordelia was getting as tired of hearing about the team's state championship prospects as she was of hearing about Steve's prowess at computer hacking.

Being steadily afflicted with the same two subjects by Ceegee, otherwise known as Charles Gordon Richardson, I could sympathize. He lives next door and has been a brother to me since our playpen days. Unfortunately, he's no longer content to be a brother. I was prepared to listen to Cordelia's wrath at having to spend two hours last night admiring Steve's practicing foul shots, in exchange for her suffering through my account of Ceegee's latest bungled attempt to be romantic. As it turned out, neither of us had much chance to air our frustrations. I did get to tell Cordelia to stop kidding herself — she'd never break up with Steve because she was besotted and she might as well admit it, and Cordelia informed me kindly that I didn't understand because I'd never been in love, and furthermore that being both a romantic and an intellectual (her words), I'd probably fall head over heels with an absolutely infuriating Adonis and fight with him all the time.

At this interesting point we beheld our "computer jocks" waiting for us on the next street corner with big pleased grins. Computer jocks — that's what Dad dubbed them a few years back when they discovered dual addictions to varsity sports and computer hacking. Dad's in no position to talk, since he goes a fair way in fitting that description himself, or used to before he became Chief of Staff at Memorial Hospital and also got involved in some highly mysterious research project, both at the same time.

When I pointed this out to Dad, he informed me that it grieved him to acknowledge that I was no athlete, but I certainly was well on the way to qualifying as a computer addict. *That* referred to the fact I was better at computer programming than he is, which gives him quite a charge. I'm better at it than Steve or Ceegee or Joe Sommers, too, but I grieve to say they do not find it amusing. They have a healthy respect for my ability, though they'd die before admitting it, but the notion that I can outprogram them does something to their macho image.

Since I'm small and blonde and deceptively helpless-looking, the jocks like to tease me that I'm too trusting, innocent, and above all straight, to ever qualify as a true hacker. We argued this point during the remaining few blocks to school, and as we scattered to homerooms the air was fraught with all the signs of a big skirmish coming, to Cordelia's great amusement. I could have wrung her neck.

The skirmish was going to be over who got what computer to work with in the school's computer lab. All of us, regardless of previous experience, were by order of the Board of Education to be afflicted with an introduction to computing course some time before graduation. Steve, who was graduating in June, could put it off no longer; the rest of us were getting it over with ahead of time. I'd already learned I was the only girl signed up for this particular class session, and I knew I'd have to fight to get to use a halfway decent computer, instead of the ones that computer illiterates had already battered — so I was going to have a battle on my hands, as Steve and Ceegee cheerfully informed me.

I had this on my mind, and was searching for some diabolical strategy, as I dashed to meet Cordelia in the school cafeteria at lunchtime. I was intercepted by a hall monitor. There was a telephone message for me in the office. Dr. Webster had telephoned, and wanted me to join him at the hospital for lunch.

I would like to be able to report that at that moment I felt a cold chill. Actually, I'm not sure. I do know this was unexpected, therefore puzzling. Dad could rarely make time for treats like this anymore. I dove into the girls' room, brushed my hair, and looped it up in a twist. If I was having a lunch date, I might as well look the part. I was glad I'd worn my new suit that made my eyes dark blue, and that I'd helped myself to Mother's beloved Art Nouveau haircomb. I emphatically did *not* feel like a cute little fluffy kitten (the image Ceegee delights in holding over me) as I sailed into the hospital and along the second floor corridor to Dad's office.

Then I caught one look at Dad himself, standing waiting in the outer doorway, and I kid you not, I really did feel a chill. Dad and the jocks love to tease me about ESP and premonitions, but I had one then.

"Dad, what's going on?" I asked, alarmed.

"Calm down," Dad advised mildly, stepping back to let me in. He didn't deny something was going on, I noticed. I also noticed his secretary for once was nowhere to be seen. "Can't I simply want to have lunch with my daughter once in a while?"

"You can, but you usually don't."

" 'Don't' doesn't mean 'doesn't want to,' necessarily." Dad led the way into his private office and I followed, my bewilderment increasing. The side table was pulled from the wall and set formally for two.

"No privacy in the cafeteria or staff dining room. I need to talk to you alone."

Dad had noticed my astonishment. That

certainly increased when he locked the door and told the switchboard operator to hold all calls. "What do you want to do first, eat or talk?" he asked me.

"If you think I can wait to hear what this is all about —"

Dad shook his head. "All business, aren't you? You even look businesslike. That ought to make this easier, but it doesn't. I'm not stalling, just having second thoughts. When I look at you and remember chasing you away from my personal computer just two years ago —"

"Dad! "

"Sorry, honey. I'm just trying to figure out where to start." Dad's teasing manner fell off like a shell. He held a chair out for me at the table and seated himself opposite. For a minute we stared at each other, then Dad asked abruptly, "Sidney, how much do you know about Project Aardvark?"

The question was so unexpected that I almost jumped. "I know you've been working on it for about four years. And that Mom named it that because aardvark's the first word in most dictionaries, and she kids you that your research is always the first thing on your mind. Dad, you didn't pull me out of school just to ask me what I know about your work!"

"I pulled you out to ask you if you would do some computer work for me on the project. Now, I'm not so sure."

"Why not?" I started to ask, indignantly.

Then caught my breath. "No, that's not the real question. Why me? Why aren't you using the hospital office staff? Or even Steve, or Ceegee? They're all doing free-lance computer work, and you absolutely refused to let me do that except during school vacations. What made you change your mind?"

"Because you're good. And because I trust you," Dad answered oddly. "And also you have some — unique attributes — that are needed. This is something that needs doing quickly, and I don't have time to screen applicants for both the peculiar aptitudes needed, *and* discretion."

My eyes narrowed. "You need someone so fast you didn't even know about it before you got here this morning? That's true, isn't it?"

"Yes, it is. And the reason I'm no longer sure about using you is that it's suddenly dawned on me that there could be a great deal of danger involved."

I felt again that shiver of alarm. I willed my voice steady. "If *you're* involved, I might as well be, too. If there's risk, don't I have the right to hear what it's all about and make my own decision?"

I knew I'd reached him. "Let's start eating," he said, and this time he *was* stalling. He went to the hot tray and served himself, and I did likewise. It wasn't till he'd plowed methodically through most of his Chinese chicken with sesame seeds that he continued.

"You know I've been working on Project Aardvark for quite a while. First in book research, then lab work. This past year, in addition to the lab work, I've been computerizing the lab tests and data on the mainframe here and on our computer at home, before we transferred it upstairs to your work station. We're right at the point of needing human research subjects to work with the hardware we've just received access to."

He said *we*, my mine noted. Just as I'd thought, he wasn't in this alone. And that reference to hardware —

"Dad" — I could be abrupt, too — "what happened today, and what does it have to do with hardware?"

"I found out this morning somebody's been tampering with the Project Aardvark computer files," Dad said bluntly. "Research has been read, or copied; maybe altered."

I didn't need a diagram drawn. Computer thefts have become big business and a major crime, with everyone from student hackers to multinational corporations involved. "How bad is it?" I asked soberly.

"Very bad. The work I've been doing doesn't just have medical implications. It has — other uses." Dad visibly checked himself. "The break-in means we — I — have to finish my work quickly, apply for patents where appropriate, and publish reports in scientific journals before the results of the research can be put to negative use."

"Dad, will you stow the scientific jargon and tell me what this is about in plain English?"

Dad regarded me gravely, and I could feel the air in the room becoming noticeably tenser. "There's another reason for the name being Project Aardvark," he said at last. "Aardvark is the first dictionary word; alpha's the first Greek letter. The project is research into the potential for communicating via alpha waves. What, if anything, do you know about alpha state?"

I stared at him. "It's an altered state of consciousness, isn't it? Like in that movie a few years ago. Or what some kids try to hit when they get stoned."

"An artificially induced chemical means to a state all humans supposedly can achieve naturally, and many do. You, for instance." Dad smiled faintly as I gave him a startled look.

"The term refers to a scientifically measurable number of cycles of electrical energy that the brain emits per second. The normally alert, rationally conscious brain has a frequency of more than fourteen cycles per second. That's beta state — what we're in right now. Alpha state is when the brain slows down to eight to thirteen cycles. That's a semi-conscious state — meditation. Or sometimes an out-of-the-body experience; sometimes a sensation of some power inside or outside ourselves taking over, working through our faculties. What sometimes happens to some actors, speakers, dancers, or musicians." He looked at me directly. "What happens to you when you psych out. And when you get your flashes of intuition."

I was getting one now. "What are the other states?"

"The next slower is theta, which is four to seven cycles per second, characterized by hallucinations or excessive anxiety. Last is delta, from one-half to three cycles, a state of deep waking-sleep. Alpha is, by all accounts, the most tranquil, and the most productive. The subject is in touch with both the inner self and the outer world."

"What does this have to do with Project Aardvark?" *And with me?* my mind added.

"It may be an explanation of mental telepathy and other forms of ESP. A scientific, provable explanation. More, it may be a means of enabling people unable to talk — for physical or other reasons — to have communication with the outside world. The mute. The autistic. The paralyzed. Those in comas. Suppose their minds, in alpha state, could communicate with a computer that could be their mouth, their eyes and ears, their hands?"

"Dad!"

"Pretty mind-boggling, isn't it?" Dad asked dryly. "But the other side of the coin is what that same computer could do in the wrong hands. Terrorists. Psychotics. Criminals. Even the military, or unfriendly governments. A computer that could read your every thought, provided you were within its radius. A computer that could brainwash *you*, aim and shoot weapons, administer drugs or poison."

I shuddered. "At least the computer that could do that hasn't been invented."

"But it has," Dr. Webster said, very quietly. "It's sitting in Hank Monahan's computer lab in the high school, right now."

For a split second, something in my brain went *click*, as though a camera lens were opening and shutting. In that instant everything was frozen, very sharp and bright. I felt as if the brown tweed pattern of the office sofa, the geometric of the curtains, the expression on my father's face, were being imprinted forever in my memory. Then my breath returned.

I asked in a dry voice, "How? Why?"

"*How* is because Monahan's an old buddy of the father of the inventor of SMN computers. And because that inventor is interested in the possibilities I just spoke of, and very concerned they don't fall into the wrong hands. *Why* is so that Project Aardvark research can be carried out."

"In the *school*?" I asked stupidly.

"Partly for protective coloring, and because SMN does have a new prototype model, the Gemini, to be tested. New high-tech products are often tested in this manner. Except that this particular Gemini has — extra features. The electromagnetic wave respondability, and theoretically the ability to give its own responses in the same manner." Dad paused. "Monahan doesn't know about the alpha features, by the way. The less people who know, the safer Project Aardvark and the computer are."

"Dad, why are you telling *me*?"

"Because I need you," Dad answered just as bluntly. "The plan was to use the usual research subjects — college and med students — people experienced in meditation. But if some other agency is tapping into Project Aardvark data in order to develop an alpha capacity computer first, there's no time to recruit subjects who would have security clearance."

He rubbed his graying beard, looking troubled. "Believe me, I'd rather try contacting the Gemini myself. But I'd waste precious time. I'm too rational; the only time I've even come close to an altered state was when I was coming out of anesthesia once. Besides, if someone is aware that the Project Aardvark work is mine, *I could* be watched, or sabotaged."

Illumination was beginning to come. "But I'm 'protective coloring,' aren't I? Young. Female. It's natural for me to be around the school." I grinned faintly. "Besides, I'm notoriously turned off by science, and have been very vocally bored lately about hacking!"

"Exactly. And I have a cover to explain your hanging around the computer lab. Your mother's finally going to get on with that cookbook she's been talking about for years.

You'll be doing the nutritional calculations, recipe analysis, and word processing for her. If the Gemini lives up to expectation, you'll be able to do some of it in alpha state. I've just arranged with Monahan, by phone, for you to be assigned to the Gemini in class and to use it after school for your mother's work. People will buy that, because the Gemini's main features are an enormous memory and compatibility with all the other major computer systems."

Monahan, former pro football star and the high school's computer teacher and head coach, was a golfing buddy of Dad's, which explained that part. As for that cookbook — "Mom knows about all this, then?" I asked.

"Your mother's known all about Project Aardvark from the beginning. She's done most of the mathematical calculations for me." Mother's a former mathematics professor who's so liberated she has no guilt pangs about having withdrawn from the workplace at a tender age.

"About my bringing you into it — she's not thrilled, but she agrees the decision must be up to you." Dad paused. "Understand this, Sidney. You can't talk about this to *anyone*, whether you take the assignment on or not. For project security and your own protection, you won't know any more about the work than is absolutely necessary. I'm not trying to frighten you unnecessarily, but it's important for you to be aware of all this before you make up your mind. I really do think that with the protective coloring, you'll be quite safe. But there are no guarantees. If your guard slips, and you say something inadvertently where the wrong ears can hear, all my work with Project Aardvark will be jeopardized. And crime-by-computer is no longer a minor offense — it's a major crime, with millions of dollars at stake. Anyone in the wrong place, at the wrong time, knowing or discovering too much, is in danger."

I wet my lips. "How long will the job take?" I asked, stalling for time.

"As long as it takes you to do the experiments and, I hope and pray, to establish regular contact with the Gemini via alpha waves. And to write me a program that will classify and analyze my research data. I was going to do that myself, but you can do it faster and most likely better. I would estimate, about a month."

There was no reason for my stalling. I'd known from when Dad first started talking what my response would be. Before I could make it, Dad pushed back his chair and strode to the window.

"I've changed my mind," he announced. "I don't want you anywhere near this whole thing!"

I did not get my stubbornness out of the clear blue sky. If my mathematical aptitudes came from Mother, my pigheadedness and response to challenges was pure Webster. I stood up, too.

"Oh, no, you don't," I announced firmly.

"I know too much already for you to let me out. Like you said, I've got protective coloring. I'll be fine. I won't say anything I shouldn't. And I guarantee to get your programming done within the month."

I was going to get the alpha contact established, also, but I didn't promise that.

I floated out of Dad's office on a little euphoric cloud and far too late to make going back to school worthwhile. It wasn't till I was a block away from the hospital that one fact hit me, like a zap from the Gemini into my subconscious.

If somebody was breaking into Project Aardvark data stored in the hospital computer, it must be someone here in Lakeland, because how else would he know about it? In which case, I wasn't going to just be a computer programmer and a research subject. I was probably going to wind up a detective-by-computer, by virtue of being allowed into Dad's data file. Courtesy of the computer jocks, I knew a lot more about the means and evidence of computer piracy than did my sheltered father. And for that very reason ... this was what made the sun-bright February afternoon turn suddenly very cold ... whatever evidence I might uncover could easily point to someone that I knew.

Chapter 2

I didn't like what I was thinking one bit.
Quite suddenly, I didn't want to deal with it.
And if you want to tell me that playing
ostrich only leaves one vulnerable to attack
from the rear, don't bother. In the first place,
I already knew it. In the second place, I was
about to have the lesson pounded home.

At that particular moment, fortunately, I
was not aware of that fact. What I was aware
of was all the bragging I'd been hearing from
Ceegee and Steve about their hacking. Oh,
they always virtuously pointed out that they
only did it for fun and information, *they*
didn't sell secrets or do malicious mischief.
But I couldn't help remembering the time last
year when Steve tried to change a D in the
school's computerized grade system to a C, so
he wouldn't be suspended from the team by
Monahan. He let gremlins loose in the machine by accident, and there was the dickens
to pay. Steve wound up with an F and three
days suspension, both courtesy of the principal, in place of the C he coveted. Since then

he'd had Cordelia coaching him in English, and checking grammar and spelling in his assignments, so he'd been getting his C's legitimately, and he swore he no longer tampered with anything when he went hacking. I only wished I could believe him.

I stood on the street corner in the February cold and contemplated what I should do now. I could go back to school and try to get Monahan to give me a crack at the SMN Gemini, but maybe Monahan would ask unfortunate questions about why I hadn't been in class. I could go home, and stew some more about hackers that I'd known. What I wanted was to preen myself on the compliment of Dad's asking me to do computer work for him, except I wasn't supposed to tell anybody about that.

I could, however, go down to the computer store where all the jocks hung out and check out the SMN models already on the market. I could drop a casual remark about working with my mother on a cookbook. I could let the guys tease me about going into competition with them as free-lancers, and remind them sweetly that their only expertise in the recipe field consisted of their devotion to devouring my mother's cooking. I wanted to hear the laughter and the teasing, and be reassured that none of the jocks could have anything to do with the Project Aardvark problem, that they were the same sweet, lovable idiots I'd idolized when I was in junior high.

Actually, I succeeded so well at this that by the time I reached the computer store the sharp afternoon sunlight had made the dark shadows lingering from my talk with Dad seem like figments of my overactive imagination. Project Aardvark couldn't really be threatened, or threatening! Apprehension faded into excitement and exhilaration at the chance of being in on this with Dad. *What could happen?* I almost laughed aloud.

The computer store was warm and steamy, smelling of wet woolens, cigarettes, and male athletes. None of the high school crowd was there at the moment, just some seventh-graders browsing through the video games and trying to sound like jocks. The store owner was keeping an eye on them, as he demonstrated the features of a new printer to a potential customer.

I detoured past them, cut around the high rack of magazines, and there it was, sitting across the way. An SMN Capricorn, the hottest and one of the most expensive personal computers currently on the market. A man in an expensive-looking coat stood to one side of it, his back to me. I scarcely saw him, because my eyes were fixed on the Capricorn. How I'd coveted one when the big media hype came out for it last Christmas season! And now a new SMN was on the way which would far surpass it, and *I* was going to be the first person outside its inventor's office to have a whack at it.

I moved toward the Capricorn greedily,

and then it happened. My foot struck something, and suddenly I was flying through the air. I landed against the man in the dark coat, ricocheted off him, and fell backwards into one of the store display cases. Piles of advertising leaflets showered from the counter. The corner of the case jabbed into my rib cage viciously.

I landed in a humiliating heap on the floor. My hair had fallen down, which meant I'd lost Mother's Art Nouveau hairpin. I reached out blindly along the floor, searching for it, and my hand encountered something hard. A burnished leather attaché case — so *that* was what had tripped me! — and peering coyly around its corner was Mother's hairpin. I started to push the attaché case away so I could reach it, and a voice said coldly, "*Do* you mind?"

He stood there, staring down at me with eyebrow raised, the man with whom I'd just had a very personal encounter. Only he wasn't a middle-aged man at all. Oh, he was very male, that much I *did* notice even in my befuddled state. But he couldn't have been more than a year older than I. His hair was wavy, and very black, and his eyes were, too, like the Mediterranean princes we've seen in Renaissance paintings. The look in those eyes made me feel like a specimen under a microscope. He wasn't very tall, not much taller than I, but he didn't seem small. He didn't seem like an athlete either. A panther, that was it — a black panther prepared to spring. Somebody who could be dangerous, something said inside my head. Only I wasn't frightened. I was far too angry.

If Mr. Superior had been one of the school crowd, he'd have grinned and held out a hand and helped me up. Not this one. He stood there, looking supercilious. Then he did reach down, only it was to move the attaché case out of my proximity, and my blood boiled.

"I was not about to walk off with that," I remarked with as much dignity as I could muster. He ignored me and turned back to the Capricorn. I was left with aching ribs and wounded pride, crawling around to pick up my books and the fallen flyers.

A gust of air and noise announced the arrival of the crowd from school and all of a sudden Ceegee was there, his amiable face sympathetic, helping me round up the debris. "Saw you through the window," he said, grinning. "I wondered if you were inventing some new kind of acrobatics."

"Thanks a whole heap." I rubbed my elbow.

"What you get for cutting Monahan's class," Ceegee retorted, hauling me to my feet. "Not to mention cutting lunch. I thought you were going to bring me some of that mocha fudge cake your mom made yesterday."

"I had lunch with Dad at the hospital."

"You really need a keeper to walk you home," Ceegee said thoughtfully, as I brushed myself off. "I could make the sacrifice. We could investigate the cake situation when we got there. Maybe discuss going to the movies Saturday night."

It was the kind of conversation we'd had many times before. Today, with the stranger standing there and hearing, it seemed — different. I summoned all my finesse and turned on a dazzling smile. "I wouldn't dream of taking you away from the videogames," I said sweetly. "Now go play with them like a good little boy, while I get acquainted with this computer."

Ceegee, taking this in the spirit in which it was intended, grinned and ambled off. I stashed Mother's hairpin in my purse and started for the SMN. Mr. Superior turned around and demanded, "Just what do you think you're doing?"

For a minute I just gaped at him. Then I drew myself up. "I'm going to try out this computer. That's what it's here for. *If* you don't mind."

"I do mind. I'm going to buy it. If I can ever get any attention." He raised his voice. "Is anyone here going to wait on me?"

"Just a minute, sonny," Mr. Sinkway called over without looking. He doesn't let the jocks push him around any more than Monahan does. I settled back to enjoy the fun. *Sonny* — I knew exactly how that made him feel, and half of me felt a sneaking sympathy. Truthfully, I expected him to walk out, but he didn't. He stood blocking the Capricorn from the world, meaning me, until Mr. Sinkway brought himself over, prepared to be tolerant of another teenage window-shopper.

"I'm buying this," Mr. Superior announced, indicating the Capricorn. Mr. Sinkway looked bored and quoted a price. Superior didn't turn a hair. He pulled out a wad of bills that would have choked a horse, and I felt a hush fall through the store. He had everybody's attention now. Even Mr. Sinkway was respectful.

"Won't have one in stock for three days. This is a demonstration model."

"I'll take it anyway. Now. I'll call a taxi to take it home in, while you pack it up. Don't let anyone touch it while I'm gone." He strode off, while I blazed.

"Good-bye, Mr. Sinkway," I said loudly, and took off myself, giving Ceegee a wide berth as I did so.

I thought I was on my way straight home, but my feet beat their customary path toward Cordelia's. I bumped into her before I got there, just getting home from another stint of watching Steve practice in the gym.

"So that's where he was. I wondered why he wasn't in the audience, too."

"What audience? Where?" Cordelia took a good look at my face. "Okay," she said wisely. "Spit it out. What happened?"

I gave her an annotated version of my encounter with a black leopard in the computer store.

"Calm down," Cordelia counseled serenely. "You don't usually get this mad when some guy who doesn't know you gets fooled by your exterior packaging and treats you like a cute little kid. You just zing him where it hurts — in the grade point average."

"This one doesn't go to our school."

"Well, he's probably going to, if he's the age you say. He must be new in town. He'll probably be in one of Monahan's classes. If you don't get to deflate his head size, the jocks sure will — especially if Ceegee just saw this afternoon's performance."

"He saw. He wanted to rescue me. I squelched him with my usual tenderness."

"He'll survive," Cordelia said dryly. "What I want to know is why this male chauvinist pig got under your skin so much this afternoon. What's he like?"

"Other than the swelled head? Black hair, black eyes. Wears clothes like a business VIP. Except for the boots. He had on very good leather boots."

"My, you did notice a lot," Cordelia murmured.

"I had a good chance to notice the boots. I was on the floor nose to nose with them, remember? Otherwise he was — I don't know — kind of creepy. Like a black cat, you know?" I was struck by a sudden recognition. He had been exactly the kind of person I *could* picture using that SMN Capricorn to commit a major crime. I shivered.

Cordelia was looking at me strangely. "Hmm," she said.

"What do you mean, 'hmm'?"

"What we were talking about this morning. About how when you fall for somebody you'll probably fight like cats and dogs. He didn't make you feel creepy — he gave you the creeps. There's a difference."

"*You* said I'd fight, *I* didn't," I said irritably. "Anyway, I don't know what you're talking about!"

"Oh, yes, you do," Cordelia said knowingly. We'd reached her house, and she paused. "Want to come in a while?"

I shook my head. "Have to get home and talk to Mom. I'm going to start data processing that cookbook she's been writing. Freelance job." It seemed advisable to put that on the grapevine.

"So your mother's decided to write a cookbook, has she? Is that why you had to leave school in such a hurry to see your dad?" The air was icy, but I suddenly felt hot, and Cordelia knew it. Her face grew serious. "You don't usually go racing out of school at lunchtime, and you don't usually act as flaky as you're doing now. Is anything wrong, Sidney? Level with me."

"Not really, I — I'm just at sixes and sevens." I forced a smile. "Why don't you come on home with me for some of Mom's latest cake?"

Cordelia shook her head. "I have the baby-sitting shift from four to six." Both her parents work, and she and her older brother Mike take turns keeping an eye on the three younger kids. "If you have more cake than you can handle, put it on the windowsill, and Ceegee will follow his nose. You can count on it. Sidney, call me if you need me, will you?"

I nodded. I stood for a moment watching Cordelia mush off through an afternoon that seemed suddenly colder, her long black hair streaming in the breeze beneath the bright red tam. Then I turned and took myself towards home. I didn't know why, but by the time I reached our own white picket-fenced colonial split-level, I was filled with apprehension. Maybe it was remembering what Dad had said about the dangers to — and in — Project Aardvark. Maybe it was the fact that the phantom hackers had taken on in my mind concrete and disturbing images. Maybe it was a few other things Cordelia had said.

I went in through the side door, which isn't really on the side but midway between the garage doors and our main front entrance. Warmth and serenity met me on the threshhold. Mother had a fire burning in the kitchen fireplace, and she was setting her Spode tea service out on the round, polished table near it. She looked up with a smile.

"You look frozen. Drop your things on the deacon's bench and sit down. You just had a phone call. Somebody saying you were recommended highly for some computer programming he needed done." Mother's eyes twinkled. "I have an idea he didn't know you were still a student. When I said you weren't here he hung up before I could get his name."

I sat down, feeling flattered. Not that I could take the job, anyway, now that I had this work for Dad which was so urgent.

I looked up to find my mother watching me, an equivocal expression on her face. "Your father called me. Twice. Once before he saw you, and once after."

"You're not thrilled about my doing the work for him, are you?"

Mother shook her head. "No, but that doesn't have to make a difference. I'm probably just being a mother hen." She poured the tea, and the fragrant steam curled up around her blonde head like a wreath. "Sometimes that project of your father's . . . spooks me."

I've always known where I get what Dad is now dignifying as my "alpha ability." I looked at Mother sharply. "Mom, do you think there's any real danger involved?"

"I don't know. There could be. I know it means a lot to your father, and your helping him means a lot to him, and I'm very proud of both of you. I'm relying on your common sense to keep you out of trouble. *Both* of you," she added with some firmness. "Your father's a brilliant scientist, but he's a babe in the woods sometimes when it comes to things like alpha waves."

Sometimes I know exactly what my mother isn't saying, and this was one of those times. Mother was afraid that *Dad*, not just his work but he himself, might be in danger because of his Project Aardvark work. Because he, unlike the two of us, didn't listen to sixth-sense warnings if logic didn't tell him there was reason to.

"It's gotten through to him loud and clear that there is some funny stuff going on around the hospital," I said, answering her unspoken comment.

"Just — be careful."

"I will. Thanks for understanding that I have to do this." I put my cup down. "Mom, if you'd been me in Dad's office this noon, what would you have said?"

"If I were you at my age, I'd have done what you did. Back when I was sixteen, I don't know whether I'd have had the courage."

It was an odd word for her to choose, and it struck me. Up till now, I hadn't thought I was doing anything particularly courageous. I pushed my cup across the table for a refill and said briskly, "Okay, let's go over those recipes I'm supposed to be programming. If I'm going under cover, I'd better make it look good. And I might as well get something accomplished on them, while I'm at it."

Mother brought out her recipe files, by which I mean the assorted shoe boxes — and worse — into which she'd been stuffing them for these past twenty years. When we'd made a good mess of the kitchen table, we adjourned upstairs to my own domain to establish what Mom called "uniform recipe styling" on a data disk.

Our household personal computer started

out being Dad's, residing in his study next to the garage, but since I started computing and he became Chief of Staff, it's moved to what I grandly call my office.

I have the whole of the house's second level — what used to be the family room, a bedroom and bath, even a tiny kitchen and a fireplace. I always feel a wave of pride and pleasure when I enter it. Today, although Mother and I were gabbing a mile a minute, there was a weighted undercurrent beneath our chatter. But by the time we'd finished conferring on the recipes, and I'd given her an unexpurgated account of my encounter with the male chauvinist pig black panther, the dark cloud had considerably lightened. When we went downstairs again to throw some dinner together, I was having intoxicating visions of myself with the SMN Gemini, being interviewed on TV maybe, a successful researcher in a white lab coat or tailored suit and upswept hair.

Dad came home for dinner for once at a decent hour, bringing a bulging, unfamiliar attaché case. "For my new assistant. It works on a combination lock, and I want you to set it for something you can't forget and no one else would ever guess. All the Project Aardvark material you're to work with is inside it, and from now on, it and you are to be Siamese twins unless it's locked up here. When you take it to school to work with at the Gemini, cleave to it until death do you part."

I held my tongue. Contemporary high school customs are one thing Dad's not too bright about. If I started carting an attaché case around the place, I'd arouse everyone's suspicion. Stashed in my locker beneath some grungy gym things, it would be completely safe. Certain things get stolen from our lockers, but attaché cases aren't among them.

Dinner over, Dad looked at me. "Want to have a conference on the material?"

"Certainly. I'll go boot up the computer." I took the attaché case, feeling deliciously professional, and went upstairs to get things going. But as I snapped the switch and the red lights blinked at me, I couldn't help wishing I owned an SMN, wishing that spectacular Gemini was right here. Not that I wouldn't settle for the Capricorn, if *I* had a wad of bills to buy one. I wondered where he'd gotten that wad. I wondered what he was doing right now — checking out all the Capricorn's expensive features, or already programming?

Why was I thinking about him, for heaven's sake? And why was Cordelia so darn smart? My face scarlet, I was just trying to figure out the locks on the attaché case when I heard the doorbell ring.

My father was opening the front door as I came out of my office to the landing. I heard a male voice, an alarmingly familiar male voice, say, "Is this where Mr. Sidney S. Webster lives? I'm J. J. Rivington III. I've come to contract him for some computing work."

My father's face was a study. He said

noncommittally, "Do come in," and stepped back. Rivington III stood in the center of our hall, in those boots and fancy coat, just as I came downstairs in *my* home-office attire, namely battered slippers, Dad's old shirt, and jeans.

If I was astonished to see him there, that was nothing to the totally satisfying effect that *my* appearance had on him. His jaw dropped. So did his superior dignity. He actually sputtered.

"*You!*"

Chapter 3

"Me," I said sweetly. "Or I could say Sidney Scott Webster. The Fourth, if you wish to get technical. I understand you want to discuss a business matter."

I sailed over to shake hands, and this time I did not trip. His hand was like a limp fish, which I suspected was not usually the case. As Mother had said, he hadn't expected Sidney Scott Webster to be a student. He also hadn't expected Sidney Scott Webster to be a female. That stuck out all over the place, and so did the ramifications of his dilemma. He wanted to get out of there, but clearly I also had something that he needed, so there he stood, uncharacteristically uncertain, clutching his attaché.

I waved a hand towards the stairs. "Won't you step up to my office?" I invited grandly, and led the way, avoiding my father's eyes.

Thank goodness I hadn't yet spread out the Project Aardvark material. Thank goodness the office looked neat and businesslike. J. J.

Rivington's eyes fell on the computer with something like relief. "You use an Apple."

"It has CP-M compatibility, and added power. It's quite satisfactory." I couldn't help adding slyly, "I was considering an SMN, but there aren't any in stock in town at the moment."

He wouldn't take the bait. His eyes were cold. "I do free-lance programming and data processing. Right now I'm backlogged because one firm in California has redesigned its project several times and is on deadline."

Translation: *You took on too much and now you're backed into a corner,* I thought. No way was I going to help him out of admitting as much. I gave him one of Dad's bland half-smiles. "What brought you to me?"

"I asked around town and was told Sidney Webster was the quickest and most reliable programmer who might be available." I could figure that one out, too. Mr. Sinkway at the computer store had sicked him on me, because he hadn't liked that overbearing manner. Mr. Sinkway was counting on me to cut J. J. Rivington III down to size, and it was going to be a pleasure. We stood there, half a room apart, like two adversaries in a prize-fight ring.

His eyes fell on the recipes still spread out on the work station, the recipe format blinking on the monitor, and his lip curled faintly. "This was a mistake. I can see you already have, er, projects —"

It was that lip curl that did it. I had been fully prepared to send him off with his deadline problem still like a weight upon him. Instead of that, my own chin lifted. I heard my own voice saying in clear crisp tones, *"I'm* quite capable of handling more than one work contract at a time. All the other free-lancers who take small jobs are tied up with a state basketball championship competition at the moment. So if your work really is urgent, Mr. Rivington, I'm afraid you're stuck with a woman programmer, whether you want that or not!"

"You did *what?*" my father demanded when I reported these developments. "Sidney, you're going to have your hands full with the work I want you for."

"I know I will. I can get his stuff done, too. It's small potatoes from the sound of it, no matter how he talks. And it will give me extra protective coloring. Besides, Dad, you didn't really expect me to let him get away with that routine he was pulling, did you?"

Dad, who had apparently heard the tale of my Round #1 with Rivington while Round #2 was going on, only shook his head. "I hope you know what you're doing," he murmured in an elaborately absent tone.

We spent the rest of the evening going over Project Aardvark material, and it was sufficiently engrossing that nothing further about J. J. Rivington III came up in conversation. I was almost able to keep from thinking about him myself.

"You **did** *what*?" Cordelia exclaimed at the lunch table, exactly as my father had done. "Sidney Webster, are you out of your mind?"

"Absolutely not. One, it will give me a respectable surface reason to be too busy when Ceegee asks me out. You know he will, and if I tell him I'm working on Mother's cookbook, he'll want to help. Two, it's a perfect opportunity to teach J. J. Rivington III a lesson, because I *am* the fastest and most reliable programmer in the school. So I can zing him where it hurts, which is what you suggested yesterday, if you remember."

"Third, you already have one job, and you'd have turned him down if it had been anybody but him, and you know it."

I ignored that. "Third, I'm going to have the use of some fantastic new computer Monahan's testing out for the company that made it. Dad arranged that, so I'd have it for the cookbook. It's supposed to be faster than lightning, so I'll be able to keep up with both jobs." It was three jobs, but she didn't know that.

Cordelia chuckled. "I know all about that new computer. I've had an earful on the subject from Steve. The jocks think it's totally unfair that you're getting to use it instead of them, because some of them are seniors. If you ask me, that cookbook of your mother's saved Monahan's neck. Can't you see him having to pick out which of the guys to let use it? *You* having it gets Monahan off the hook and saves their pride. Plus Monahan's probably scared to death they'd wreck the thing. It's a demonstration model here on loan, isn't it? You know what happens when our geniuses decide they could improve on a computer's innards!"

I had vivid memories of computer chips and wires spread all over the Richardsons' family room. The thought of a similar fate befalling the Gemini made me shudder.

I tried to sweet-talk Heller Hazzard, the ex-minor league baseball player who's now one of our gym teachers, into letting me out of the cafeteria to the computer lab, but he was taking his responsibilities as cafeteria monitor very seriously that day and turned me down. So it wasn't till the next to the last period that I got to see the Gemini. That was my section of the introduction to computers course, which it turned out Ceegee and Steve and Joe Sommers were all in. Intro comp for most of us was a big farce, but the Board of Education had finally come down with high-tech mania. Considering that fifty percent of the class considered itself experts and another fifty percent (somewhat overlapping) were buddy-buddy with Monahan anyway, the place was bedlam. This was compounded by the fact that the whole class except for me was male. The usual whistles and cracks greeted my appearance. I took them in the spirit in which they were intended and waved them off.

I couldn't wave off Monahan, who stood between me and the Gemini, giving me the evil eye. If Dad had told Monahan *he* was responsible for my missing class yesterday, Monahan didn't show it. His famous bushy gray eyebrows beetled above his licorice-drop black eyes. I meekly presented my excused-absence pass and followed Monahan's pointed finger to the room's back corner.

There it was, the SMN Gemini, a pristine, pearly-white machine. I headed for it greedily and booted up. It responded like a dream. I was happily getting a few practice swipes made at a data base for Dad's material when I heard the sound of boots approaching.

J. J. Rivington III was bearing down on me purposefully with the light of battle in his eye. "Don't interrupt me," I said absently. "I'm concentrating."

"You're concentrating on *my* machine."

"Yours!" I yelped. "Look, Mr. Rivington Three, you may have an SMN at home, but for the duration of our class period and after school, this baby's mine."

"No, it's not," he said decidedly. "I have special arrangements to use it for my work."

"So do I!"

We glared at each other, as Monahan's dulcet tones came floating to us over all the other heads. "Two students per computer, you know that, Webster. What do you think this is, some blooming rich kids' school? Put up with each other. That's an order."

Neither one of us was going to break that eye contest first. It was broken by Ceegee who came strolling over to stand between us. "Looks like this is going to be an interesting semester," he observed with a twinkle.

For three days, there was no open warfare, only the guarded peace which precedes hostilities. Joshua J. Rivington III, however much a stranger to us up till now, was officially registered in school as a new student. In the cafeteria and the computer room, there were ribald comments at his expense, but they died at his entrance. This was partly because, by the end of the second class period, he had established himself as a computer master.

Partly it was for the reason that Ceegee confided sheepishly over the remains of Mother's fudge cake that afternoon. "Darn it, Sid, when that guy turns that quarter-smile on me, I feel like I did the first time I was yanked into the principal's office for cutting class!"

"Oh, well, computer freaks come in all kinds," I murmured. I knew the awesome proportions of the high school gossip network, and had no desire to have bets made on which of us would win the battle for the Gemini. Ceegee shot me a look.

"Wonder how you're going to get along,

working for the guy," he said innocently.

"How did you —" I caught myself. "Oh. Cordelia."

"Telling Cordelia anything's like publishing it in the *Lakeland Gazette*," Ceegee agreed, grinning. "You're not *that* hard up for things to do, from how you tell it."

"He implied I wasn't up to the level of his precious work, and of course I rose to the bait. Anyway," I added hastily, "it's good practice for me on the Gemini. Because I *do* have a lot of work, as you just reminded me."

On Tuesday evening J. J. Rivington III spent an hour and a half in my office, laying out the work he wanted me to handle. It was pretty dull, an inventory control system for a hardware firm. I could tell exactly the mess he'd gotten himself into. He'd taken on too much work, and promised it in too short a time. And he was burdened with a client who had changed his mind four times already about what he wanted. It looked to me as if that client was driving Rivington crazy, and as if that very fact was driving him even crazier. After the first half hour that Tuesday night, it was very clear that my esteemed employer didn't like being in situations he could not control.

After he left, I put in two solid hours on Dad's Project Aardvark work. I could do ordinary data processing for that at home, but my fingers itched to get at the special features of the SMN in school. Especially the alpha experiments. The data Dad had given me to work with seemed at first as dull as that hardware stuff had been, but by the time I put the computer and me to bed at nearly midnight, I was starting to get hooked.

On Wednesday, after ten minutes of fielding arguments from the computer jocks and Josh, Monahan let loose a bellow. "Now hear this! I *know* a lot of you are already computer literate! You're not geniuses on *all* machines. You're not geniuses on self-discipline. You will all complete every assignment that I give, whether you consider it rinky-dink and beneath your talents or not. *After* each assignment's on my desk, you can use the rest of the class period for your own computer purposes. Not before, and no exceptions. I'm willing to consider some of 'your own work' for extra credit, but only if it meets my standards and your class work is done. Got that?"

Rivington's face tightened, and Steve and Ceegee went through a few gripes for appearance's sake. I just said, "Yes, sir," and was rewarded with one of Monahan's ironic looks. I couldn't very well haul out Project Aardvark, let alone practice ESP with a computer, during a class period anyway.

I wasn't supposed to be getting psychic with the SMN yet anyway, not till I'd taken a battery of scientific tests. The first group of these took place in the psychology labs of the university on Wednesday afternoon. Dad set these up, supposedly for some scholarly paper he was writing. Along with several college students, I went through a lot of experiments, trying to "pick up" which playing card a student in another room had drawn out of a deck. I felt thoroughly silly, and it didn't work.

Wednesday evening was a repeat of Tuesday's, and Thursday was a repeat of Wednesday's, right down to the unsuccessful experiments. I walked home along the shore of the lake for which our town is named, feeling thoroughly demoralized.

In summer, the lake is a haven for children, ducks, and swans. Right now it should be good for skating, but the ice was snow-covered and uneven. I plowed through snow-drifts to my favorite spot, a stone seat built into a curve of shore beneath a willow, brushed snow off it, and sat down to wrestle it out with my foul mood.

I was disgusted; I was disappointed; I was disillusioned. Disgusted with myself because I had begun to realize I'd been building up a fantasy of what all this exciting computer free-lancing would be like. I'd fallen in love with the element of danger at which Dad had more than hinted. Only there hadn't been any danger or exciting work (disappointment). There hadn't been any scientific proof of my intuition or ability to get into an alpha state (disillusion).

Capping all this was the status quo between me and Rivington and Rivington's so-important top secret work. If there was anything top secret about the work Rivington had doled out to me, I'd eat the printouts! I wasn't being challenged; he wasn't depending on me for expertise; I wasn't proving anything to him. He was only turning over to me the routine work he probably regarded as beneath him.

This thoroughly infuriated me. I sat there hammering a snowball into a ball of ice, and finally the ridiculous aspects of the situation struck me. Here I was, totally committed to really important work for my father, taking on something else just to call a male chauvinist's bluff, and then complaining that I didn't have enough to do! I started to laugh, which made me feel a little better . . . but not much.

What was *really* bothering me was that the SMN Gemini itself, not just those parapsychology tests, wasn't turning out to be as easy to work with as I had expected. The only solace was that J. J. R. III didn't seem to be doing any better himself. "I can't get a handle on the thing!" I blurted to Cordelia during Friday lunch. Cordelia didn't know computers, but she did know me.

"You're not seeing the trees for the forest," she advised comfortably. "You're great on seeing the whole picture, and what lies beneath it. Computers don't work like that, do they?" She grinned reminiscently. "Remember last year in geometry? You drove everybody crazy because you'd do the end of a problem first, *then* you'd go back and fill in all the steps. And the teacher couldn't say a word because your proofs always made logical sense."

Cordelia was right, wasn't she? *I* might know the end result intuitively, but the computer didn't, not till I'd taught it how to get there step by step. Definitely, the thing to do was slow down (a little) and think those steps through like a scientist. Computing wouldn't be painfully slow once the programs were set up. Very well, then. Until I established mastery of the Gemini — in all senses — it would be the rationalist approach all the way.

Thus fortified, I sailed into the computer lab and found J. J. Rivington III already in possession.

"Don't you ever eat lunch?" I inquired acidly.

Rivington didn't even bother looking up. "If you eat a big enough breakfast, you don't need lunch. Midday junk food only makes people sluggish and cuts down on afternoon productivity. Hand me that sheet of paper I dropped, will you, Webster?"

To my annoyance, I stooped for it before I could stop myself. Then I took a good look at it. "Where did you get *this*?"

"It's the assignments for next Thursday's and Friday's class periods. I've already finished Monday through Wednesday's. Mr. Monahan left his assignment book on his desk, so I copied out the assignments and got started. You can print out a completed copy for each of us as needed, and I'll be able to use next week's class periods for more important things. You can do the work you're doing for me, unless you have any other priorities."

I counted to ten. "Yes, I do," I said carefully. "The class assignments, just for starters."

He looked genuinely startled. "I thought lab partners worked as a team. The rest of the class does."

"You just hit the operative word. *Team.* I'm not about to be your girl friday, and I'm quite capable of doing work on the Gemini myself. I don't know where you come from, Mr. Rivington the Third, but around here team play means exactly that. Nobody coasting on somebody else's effort — and nobody having a monopoly on the ball!" I stopped. "But I suppose you think things like the basketball team, and winning a state championship, is a waste of time too, don't you?"

"Games." Rivington's lip curled slightly, and his gaze strayed to Steven and Ceegee, who at that moment were mapping out basketball strategy on an Apple II.

"You needn't be so patronizing!" I snapped. "Ceegee and Steve are both counting on athletic scholarships to help with college. It takes the same kind of mind to understand the structure of a game that it does to understand the innards of a computer program. Or a computer itself! And a grasp of team playing is essential for anyone who hopes to succeed in the real world." I had picked up that tidbit from my father. "Success with a capital $ matters to you, doesn't it? Then maybe you'd better brush up on your sportsmanship, because it sure is lousy now!"

Rivington's face went white. "Excuse me," he said stiffly. He snapped his data disk out of the Gemini and vacated his seat. I sat down, breathing hard.

"You mentioned other priorities. One of them is a project I'd already contracted myself for before you arrived on my doorstep the other night. It's important. More important than the routine work I've been doing for you, so I'm going to resign on that. You don't really need me for it, anyway. The hardware inventory program's almost finished. I'll finish that, but then that's it."

I'd rattled him, and it showed. "I told you —"

"You told me you needed someone trustworthy for a top secret project. There's nothing top secret about the stuff you've shared with me. Either you *don't* trust me with it, or you're hanging onto it for yourself — if there ever *was* anything to it. Other than a lot of hot air to make you look important!" I thrust a data disk into the Gemini so violently that the monitor blinked a protest.

Rivington immediately reached out to correct the situation. Out of concern for the SMN, not for me, of course. "I can do it myself!" I snapped. "For your information, I've been hacking since I was eleven! I can understand a computer's operating system even if I don't have an SMN of my own at home. Just what entitles you to patronize all the rest of us?"

Rivington just stood there for several minutes. When he did speak, his voice was very different — hoarse and strained. Not hostile.

"Are we going to have a fencing match, or are we going to get those class assignments done?"

"I'm going to get them done. You're going to check them." I settled before the monitor and looked over what he'd done already. It was not hard to pick up where he left off. When I stole a glance he had drawn up a chair and flopped down into it. He rubbed a hand across his eyes, caught my glance, and grimaced.

"Headache?"

"Kind of."

He looked like it was killing him to admit it. I murmured so none but he could hear, "You could put headphones on. Nobody'll know they're dead. And nobody'll know your eyes are closed if you hide behind a notebook. I have aspirin, if you want."

"Won't do much good," he mumbled. I nodded and turned my attention to the SMN. It was performing as advertised — faster than a speeding bullet."

Rivington wasn't keeping up an act at the moment. I wouldn't have thought Mr. Cool in his three-piece suit would let himself look that way in front of the rest of us. Maybe for once he couldn't help it. I shot a glance at him, and found him watching me with a bloodshot but not particularly antagonistic eye.

"Think you'll live?" I inquired sympathetically.

He eased himself up in his chair and considered. "I'm not sure I want to."

"Up till all hours playing with your new toy?" I meant his Capricorn.

"You got it. But it wasn't playing, and it wasn't fun." He cleared his throat. "What you said before — maybe I deserved some of it. But you had one thing wrong. No, two. I do trust you. And I do need your assistance. I hope you'll reconsider about working with me."

That was handsome of him, particularly since it was obviously hard for him to say. I shook my head.

"Thanks, but I — I guess I was doing a wrong thing, too. I only took the job in the first place to prove something." I didn't add, *to you*, but he knew what I meant, and his face reddened. "That was dumb, because I really did — *do* — have an important freelance project I've hired on to do for someone else."

"The cookbook?"

I didn't answer. "So you won't reconsider?" Rivington said at last.

"No. I'm sorry," I said firmly. And spent the rest of the day wondering why I felt regretful.

Chapter 4

"It doesn't make sense!" I told Cordelia vehemently.

Cordelia wrinkled her forehead. "What doesn't?"

It was Saturday night, and we were drowning our sorrows in an orgy of hot chocolate and brownies in my office. A previously scheduled movie double date with Steve and Ceegee had been displaced by their last-minute desire to check out a rival basketball team's skill. Cordelia had had more than enough of Steve's tournament obsession for the moment, and I wasn't going to go with Ceegee if it wasn't a double date. By ten p.m. our irritation had spread from Steve and Ceegee to male chauvinists in general. I had cited Rivington as a prime example.

"Nothing about him makes sense," I elaborated, reaching for another brownie. "Doesn't add up, I mean. His clothes, for starters. That Mr. VIP overcoat, which I bet is cashmere, and the three-piece suits."

"Oh, *those*." Cordelia looked amused. "He's trying to prove something, that's all. And at least it's a change from Ceegee's Army surplus wardrobe."

"But what's he proving? That he has the guts to go to high school in a three-piece suit? It could be guts; it could be he's just plain dense."

"That I doubt."

"I don't mean stupid, I mean — impervious to reactions. And I doubt that, too."

Cordelia laughed. "Don't you mean he's trying to prove he's above the reactions of the unwashed masses? Which I have to admit Ceegee often is. Unwashed, I mean. You know how Ceegee's mind gets so wrapped up in trying to crack a secret password, or whatever the hackers call it, that he just doesn't notice mundane things like mud or axle grease. Maybe Rivington's mind is like that in a different way."

"I can believe it. And I can believe he wants people to believe that." I frowned. "Darn it, Cordelia, I just don't buy that there's anything about the man that's not deliberately planned. I told you how he looked at me that day, with his left eyebrow raised. I'll bet you anything he practiced that before a mirror. And the name! J. J. Rivington III, now I ask you!"

"Actually, it's Joshua J. Rivington III," Cordelia said demurely. I burst out laughing.

"You haven't found out what the middle J's for yet?"

"I will," Cordelia said, unruffled. "He's not in your grade, you know. He's our age, but he's a junior. And he's taking three senior-level subjects.

I sat up straight. "Cordelia, you looked him up in the office files!"

"I work in the office one period a day, don't I?" Cordelia said innocently. "Can I help noticing things when I'm filing?" Her tone sobered. "Or getting worried about a diabolical stranger when my best friend starts falling for him and working for him?"

"I'm not falling for him. And I'm not working for him. I quit."

"Now you're showing signs of intelligence," Cordelia said fervently.

Over the weekend the sleet stopped and the world became a sparkling landscape of crystal trees. I spent Sunday feeding information into the data file I'd been developing for Project Aardvark, and wishing I could get my hands on the Gemini. When I arrived in school on Monday, Monahan flagged me down in the hall.

"You can use the Gemini outside of class time up to eight hours a week. Although what's so special about a bunch of recipes that you have to do them on that particular computer, I do not see," he added sourly. "You'll have to schedule the hours you're going to use it in advance with me. And any work that faculty or administration needs done on the Gemini takes precedence. Provide your own disks, **don't** let anyone else into the classroom unless they have a pass from me, and you know you're not allowed to use the school's access to the mainframe or any outside data banks."

"Yes, sir," I murmured. I would need to plug into national data banks for some of the Project Aardvark work, but Dad had his own access numbers which I could use. I hadn't brought the Project Aardvark material to school with me, but at three o'clock I ran home for the attaché case.

The deserted computer lab was still and peaceful, filled with a dull gray light. I flipped on the high tensor lamp at the work station, leaving the overhead flourescents off, and the station became a pool of light. The Gemini hummed, and I sat silently, watching the flickering dot of glowing red that indicated all its systems were functioning. It was like a beautifully mannered litttle racehorse, raw power deceptively cloaked in sleek elegance.

The red light blinked off. The Gemini waited. I reached into the unlocked attaché case . . . then, in the act of bringing out the notebook of unprocessed data, I suddenly stopped. As if of their own volition, my hands began searching for the instructions for tapping into Gemini's "special features."

The first step was simple. Write a program. Thank goodness the Gemini was user-friendly; that meant I could use plain English, not a special language, and could develop a program in a few simple steps. And the Gemini "spoke" many computer languages as well, so I could borrow symbols, if I wished, as a kind of shorthand.

So far, so good. What now? A password. A secret code word, easy for me to remember but not too easily guessed at by outsiders. Then, if alpha communication worked, no one else could hack their way into my file. A code word was rather like a touchstone — that magical object alchemists of old used to separate fool's gold from real.

My fingers typed T O U C H S T O N E into the Gemini's memory.

The red light blinked. It was almost hypnotic, there in the tranquil room. I stared at it, watching the little beam go *on - off - on - off* in the dimness. I could feel my mind drifting, reaching out. *Drift with it,* I thought, the way a tired swimmer drifts relaxed on the crest of a wave.

Answer me, a voice in my mind seemed to call. *Touchstone, calling SMN Gemini . . . answer me. . . .*

There was a current in the room, separate and distinct from the humming motor of the quiet white machine. I could almost feel it, and it did not frighten me. It was simply *there.* Not responding, not refusing, simply waiting.

A door opened behind me, and then slammed, and the classroom was flooded with cold flourescent light. I spun around, shocked out of wherever I had been.

"Sidney — Webster, isn't it? What are you

doing here?" The gym teacher, Heller Hazzard, stood there, frowning. He was in a sweat suit, swinging a bunch of keys from one tanned hand. "No students are supposed to be in labs at this hour without a teacher in attendance."

"I have Mr. Monahan's permission." My voice, to my own annoyance, came out cracked.

"Do you have a pass?" I shook my head. "Okay, I'll check it out with Mr. Monahan tomorrow. Now you'd better beat it. It's nearly six, I have some team statistics to post on the computer, and I don't want anyone around distracting me."

I obeyed, locking the attaché case, and remembering at the last moment to retrieve my system and data disks from the SMN. I took a swift look around to make sure I hadn't overlooked anything else, and edged out, my heart pounding.

There were only six blocks to my house, and by the time I reached the last my legs felt like jelly. It was so strange. I hadn't done anything wrong. I had had a right to be in the lab, and I certainly wasn't afraid of Mr. Hazzard. But all the same I felt queer, and scared. I was very glad to see Ceegee's lanky form silhouetted against the brightness of his own garage. "Sid, for gosh sake, what's wrong with you? You look as though you'd seen a ghost!"

"I'm cold, that's all." My teeth were chattering. Ceegee appropriated my books and walked me to the door.

"Go in and warm up and stop looking at so many scary late-night movies." Ceegee opened the door and returned my belongings. "Don't bother saying thanks, but you could invite me to dinner if you feel inclined. Ma's working tonight."

"Don't you know how to warm up frozen dinners?" I inquired automatically, but I did not protest when he followed me inside. Mother, with a knowing smile, promptly extended the invitation he'd been angling for. Actually, I was glad to have Ceegee there. He wasn't being mushy; it felt as if we'd turned back the clock to a less complicated time. My father arrived, and a long technical discussion of the latest videogame technology ensued. There was something oddly comforting about the companionship and warmth, and talk that had absolutely nothing to do with Project Aardvark or alpha waves.

The name of Joshua J. Rivington III emerged. Ceegee had had a run-in with him in class that day, and was looking for some sympathy.

Dad's eyebrows rose. "It couldn't possibly be that the fellow knows more about hacking than you do, could it, Ceegee?"

Ceegee was indignant. "When I was able to get into Woodbridge High's sports records and alter the statistics of two of their prime jocks?"

"Shut up," Dad advised mildly. "You're telling things I'm better off not knowing. I stand corrected, Charles Gordon, sir. You're a veritable Robin Hood of hackers."

I heard my own voice say, in an odd tone, "Josh is good. He's very good. Maybe he has a right to be conceited."

Afterwards, I was no more sure what made me say that than I was sure what had been happening in the computer lab directly before Heller Hazzard's unexpected entrance.

Chapter 5

Lunch periods in our cafeteria are always hectic, particularly since there are more people than there are chairs. Enterprising students who finish bolting down lunch in the first ten minutes can finesse passes to the art room, shop, the school newspaper office, and other points of interest. Not the least among these is the computer lab. Since Monahan put his foot down about no more than two students getting passes there during any one period, I was becoming adept at beating the jocks to the draw.

On the day after my almost-alpha-contact with the SMN, I allowed a judicious five minutes of lunch period to elapse before sprinting to the supervising teacher to be signed out. It happened once again to be Mr. Hazzard. He signed with a flourish and flashed a smile.

"You're through lunch early! From the looks of you, you eat like a bird."

I smiled sweetly and refrained from mentioning the sandwiches snuggled next to the computer printouts in my attaché. Eating in classrooms is against the rules, but Monahan looks the other way unless debris is left around. When I got to the computer lab, Josh was there, hunched over the Gemini. He looked up as I approached, all set to bristle.

"You trying to get some work done in peace and quiet, too?" I made my voice deliberately amiable.

"Trying to get tomorrow's assignment done."

I fished my class data disk out of its file envelope. "Work from mine."

"I'm quite capable of doing my own."

"Nobody said you're not," I said patiently. "We're lab partners, aren't we? Monahan doesn't expect *both* of us to do the nitty-gritty. We just have to each turn in our own evaluations of our program, and recommendations for improving it." I slid my data disk into the Gemini. "Team work, remember? I'll run through the program while you read it. There's no point in either of us wasting computer time."

Instead of arguing, Josh squinted at the screen and started scribbling rapid notes. After a few minutes he stopped and rubbed his eyes.

"I suppose you didn't eat any lunch?" He didn't answer. I unlocked my attaché case and took out the sandwiches. "Here. Mother always insists on making me more than I can eat."

"I'm not hungry."

"Eat anyway." I unwrapped one of the sandwiches and took a thoughtful bite. "It's pretty good. Eat. It's no wonder you get headaches if you make a habit of skipping meals."

Josh unwrapped the other sandwich, took a wary bite, and a look of surprised respect crossed his face. "This *is* good. Horseradish and sour cream, isn't it? With a trace of coriander?"

My jaw dropped. "How did you come to recognize that combination?"

"How did you come up with that combination in the first place?"

"I didn't. Mother did. She's a gourmet chef. Result of all the traveling our family does. Other people come home with souvenirs. She comes home with recipes." I took another bite. "You're right, this is one of her better experiments. Just as well, considering the main ingredient is beef tenderloin! A disaster would have been what my dad would call 'not cost efficient.' "

Josh didn't laugh; he still looked intrigued. "What is your mother, a caterer? Cooking teacher? Food writer?"

"She hopes to be. If I ever get her recipes computerized." It felt so strange to be having a perfectly ordinary conversation with Rivington — and about gourmet foods, of all imaginable subjects! "How come you know so much about gourmet cooking?"

"I like to mess around in the kitchen when I have time. So you're computerizing recipes. Is that why you grab the Gemini every chance you can?"

"Uh-huh," I said vaguely. "Among other things."

In class that day Josh made no mention of our having shared an unorthodox lunch together, but I detected a definite thaw in the air. Since I was feeling mellow I let Josh have the Gemini to finish his assignment write-up, and he even said thanks as he handed the program back to me. He pushed his luck, of course, by promptly loading the Gemini up with one of his own work projects, and in the interest of sweet harmony I let him. I had plenty of nonterminal work to keep me busy, anyway.

Josh hammered away erratically for a time. Then he zapped out a whole page of work and swore.

"Stuck?" I asked, striving for Dad's carefully neutral tone.

"I can't concentrate with somebody reading over my shoulder," he said shortly.

"I'm not reading over your shoulder," I said inaccurately. "If you don't mind my saying so, you're doing an awful lot of deleting. Maybe you could use somebody else horning in."

"You have better things to do. And I'm not a team player. Remember?" There wasn't as much force as usual in his voice, and he rubbed his eyes.

"Let me see." He didn't stop me as I scrolled back to the previous page of data. "What is this, anyway?"

"Program for making correlations between chemical components. It's for a pharmaceutical firm that needs a fast way to determine allergic reaction potential in specific cases. I have all the data banked already. This is the part where I have to set up the program to draw conclusions."

At least it was in a language that I knew, even if it was chemistry, which I find a total turn-off. I studied the screen for a few minutes. Then I said, "May I?" and started rattling keys.

It was one of those times when everything seems to fall into place, as if the computer itself was helping. "Is this more or less what you're after?" I asked at last.

Josh opened his eyes and stared at the screen. He pulled in closer and stared again. Then he turned abruptly. "Where did you get that from?"

I shrugged. "I don't know. It just came. It's what you wanted, isn't it? The shortest way to get accurately from A to Z?"

Josh looked as if he couldn't believe his eyes. "It just — 'came to you'? You didn't work it out logically?"

"No. But it proves out logically, doesn't it?"

I knew darn well it did, and so did he. I'd

shaken some of the things he most surely believed, and we both knew it. I savored the sweet triumph when I saw Josh's hand shoot out to store the program before any gremlins in the Gemini could devour it. There was an awkward pause, then he cleared his throat.

"Do you mind if I use this? Of course, I'll pay —"

I waved a hand grandly. "Take it. It's worth it to hear you admit that intuition has its own logic. Not to mention proving that team work and reading over shoulders does have uses."

For a minute he just looked at me. Then, incredibly, he started to laugh. The sound started somewhere deep inside, and rusty, as if it wasn't often used. And then it burst out and bubbled over, while I stared stupefied and then cracked up, too. We stood there, the two of us, hugging our sides and looking like absolute idiots. And it was a good thing the room was so noisy, and divided into private areas by work stations, or we would have been the object of a lot of notice.

Josh had a nice laugh. He stopped at last, and wiped his eyes, and shook his head, and a lot of iron had gone out of that suit of three-piece armor. "Feel better?" I inquired demurely.

Josh looked bemused. "I don't know whether it's burnout or the headache." He shook his head, and started laughing again.

"Anyone but you, I'd say it was slap happy," I said dryly. "They don't put laughing gas in computers, do they?"

He got himself under control at last and sat down weakly. "You're not a fencer, are you, by any chance?"

I blinked. "What on earth made you ask that?"

"Because you sure know how to parry and thrust." He glanced at the monitor. "About the program — thanks a lot. Really. I'll make it up to you somehow, I promise."

It was all so unexpected, coming from him, that I couldn't think of a parry or a thrust. I managed what I hoped was an effective Mona Lisa smile, and then the bell rang, and Josh went dashing off.

"He said thank you. He actually said thank you," I muttered, gathering my belongings and wandering dazedly out into the hall.

"Who said thank you?" Ceegee demanded, falling in beside me.

"Rivington. Can you believe it?" I was so bemused by this that I scarcely noticed Ceegee taking possession of my junk and me as I headed for my last class. *Joshua J. Rivington III . . . why was I having so many dialogues in my head on that subject?* I wondered. Cordelia would have all too readily supplied a reason. I knew exactly what that reason would be, and I didn't want to contemplate it. I did something that was more than a little unfair instead. I turned a smile on

Ceegee and invited him to tell me how the team was progressing on its march to the championship.

That took till we arrived at my next classroom. Ceegee, his circuits loaded with nothing more devious than how to get into the school's mainframe and improve his grades there, was a relief after Rivington's disturbing presence.

What I should have taken into consideration was that Ceegee had a lot more he wanted to say to me than the four minutes between classes allowed time for. When school let out I found him at my locker, with every intention of walking me home. I got hold of Cordelia and dragged her with me to the girls' room.

Cordelia was unsympathetic. "If you didn't want to start something, you shouldn't have encouraged him. I know you're supposed to be a genius, girl, but there are times when you are not quite bright."

"I'm not a genius," I said shortly. "I'll fix things up with Ceegee as soon as I can. But not now. I've really got to work in the computer lab, and I have to work alone. Please, Cordelia!"

Cordelia regarded me thoughtfully. "Okay, I'll head him off for now," she said at last. "But you do have to get some things straightened out. And I don't mean with your darned computers. Are you really sure how you feel about that precious lab partner of yours?"

She left while I was still speechless.

I hid out in the girls' room for fifteen minutes, improving the time by getting some homework done while I was waiting. When I emerged, the corridor was deserted, except for the new janitor. Higgins, or Wiggins, or something like that, his name was.

Monahan was still in his office, but about to leave. "If you want special privileges, you can at least come on time," he said acidly. "I was just ready to lock up."

"I'm really sorry. It won't happen again."

Monahan grunted, but beneath his bushy brows his eyes had a wry twinkle. "Better not. Any other day, you'd have lost your computer time to your esteemed lab partner."

"Why not today?"

"You haven't found out yet? He's taking advanced classes at the university. Keep that under your lid. The kid thinks nobody here knows about it." Monahan started to leave, then paused. "By the way, I heard about Mr. Hazzard kicking you out the other day. He knows now that you're authorized. Just remember, a teacher posting records in the school mainframe does have priority over kids' own projects." He made his exit.

So Rivington took college courses but wanted to keep it quiet. That didn't fit with what I'd have expected, and made me think better of him.

There I was, thinking about Joshua J. Rivington III again.

I marched myself firmly to the Gemini, booted up, and stared at it. I could have sworn it was watching me mockingly. It ran through its little humming routine, and its red lights blinked.

INSERT DATA DISK, the monitor ordered in luminous green letters.

"You can talk. Why don't you say it out loud," I responded crossly. I hadn't gotten around to trying its voice-command features yet. It would take time to program the computer to respond to my voice patterns, and to *them* only. So far, I had merely fed in the identity code for alpha wave communication. *If* such communication really was possible.

All at once, I wanted to get on with it. This afternoon the school was still. But the room was bright. I switched on my tensor lamp; crossed to flip off the ceiling lights. The room became thick with shadows. I slipped the same data disk in the machine, typed in the answers I had keyed to the command that sprang to light upon the screen, typed in the code word: T O U C H - S T O N E.

Nothing happened. I stared until the letters swam, but could not clear my mind. That conversation with Cordelia, the earlier one with Josh, kept intruding with disturbing implications.

Get back to the touchstone, not just the key word but my own personal touchstone, which was that I *am* good at computing. Not a genius, as Cordelia had teasingly accused, but *good*. Good enough to make mental contact with this machine? I concentrated hard, but nothing happened. Not the way it had yesterday. What had I done then that I wasn't doing now?

Maybe it wasn't anything I had *done*.

There has to be something — or some routine — the operator can do to establish contact, I thought doggedly. *Otherwise it's all too chancy.* For Project Aardvark to have practical applications, as Dad hoped, there had to be a way to program the human as well as the machine.

That was the problem, wasn't it? Maybe this SMN was all geared up for that special kind of programming, but Sidney Scott Webster wasn't — yet. I had to learn more first — not about programming, but about brain waves and the alpha state.

I ought to be putting in time in the library, not here, I concluded with exasperation.

Okay, if my brain was firmly fixed in a rational state of mind today, I might as well take advantage of it and do some programming. I switched data disks, then checked the files. That's one of the things Monahan hammers into us — always be sure to file your work; always make back-up copies; always check the files to make sure the gremlins haven't gotten in. Even a machine like the Gemini could have gremlins.

The programming and data I'd already filed on this disk for my father was secure. I switched to the Gemini's own memory system, punched in the signals for EDIT and

FIRST BLANK PAGE, and settled down to work.

The classroom buzzer sounded shrilly.

I jumped, my hand skittering across the keys. Then I relaxed. The school building's old, and short circuits in the wiring are not uncommon. *Just so the short's not in the line leading to this computer*, I thought, relieved. Although actually that wouldn't be catastrophic, either. The Gemini had its own memory system which retained an enormous quantity of most recently processed material, even if not yet filed. It retained it for up to twenty-four hours, even if the current was shut down.

I turned back to the monitor, ready to work, and did a double-take. My fingers, jumping as I had jumped, had produced a string of gibberish on the screen.

No, not just gibberish. The symbols, alphabetic, algebraic, and graphic, repeated themselves in orderly progression, and there were too many repeats for them to have been entered merely by my straying fingers. I squinted at them with vague curiosity. Then, my curiosity was wiped out and replaced with something sick and cold.

Glaring at me out of the unintelligible code phrases on the screen were two phrases that in the past week had become as familiar to me as my own name. They were variants of physics formulas, the result and core of my father's work on Project Aardvark.

Chapter 6

For a moment, I simply stared. Then, instinctively, I pushed FILE. Within seconds all the gibberish from the screen was stored on my data disk. I retrieved it again and began scrolling with mounting tension. There were a total of six pages in which Dad's formula appeared. Beyond that, there was nothing except the data I myself had filed the last time I worked.

There was only one explanation. Those six pages had to have come out of the machine's own twenty-four-hour memory, and somebody else had put them there. Somebody else was computing with Project Aardvark data, and must have done it just before I booted up the machine; that meant during the last period of the school day, when no class was taking place in the lab, or right after school, during the time I was avoiding Ceegee.

There were footsteps in the hall outside. Automatically my fingers pushed the button to clear the screen.

The footsteps stopped, right outside the door. The door did not open. It must be the custodian. Or Hazzard, with his basketball stats. Or Monahan, coming back. Only why didn't they come in?

Very casually, I put all my work away in the attaché case, snapped the locks, and turned, under pretext of stretching, towards the door.

There was no one there. No shadow against the smoked glass of the door's half-window; no face in the clear pane. I turned back towards the computer, and remembered the disks still in the disk drive slots. I should make back-up copies. I should unlock the attaché case and put the disks inside, under lock. But suddenly I didn't want to be in that room another moment. I thrust the disks inside my notebook, praying they wouldn't be damaged, snapped off the computer, and started for the door with feet that felt like lead. My heart was pounding as I opened the door.

Josh was standing at a locker not four feet away, his back to me. He was not at the university where he was supposed to be. The door had whined as I opened it, but he did not turn. He could have been carved in stone.

I let the door swing shut behind me and started in the opposite direction down the hall. My shoes squeaked on the floor's waxed surface, but I went at a deliberately normal pace. It was not till I was downstairs, within

ten feet of the exit door, that I allowed myself to run.

Night had closed in. I reached home to find
a fire burning in the kitchen fireplace and
mouth-watering odors coming from the stove.
Everything was so normal that I felt immediately soothed. I was also relieved to find that
Ceegee wasn't underfoot.

"He came home from basketball practice
half an hour ago, but he hasn't been around."
Mother had correctly interpreted my glance
towards the window. "Are you two on the
outs? I felt sure he'd drop in because his
folks aren't home, so he's on his own for
dinner."

"I just don't want him to get ideas I don't
have. Mom, is Dad home?"

"I think I just heard his car. Set the table,
will you, darling?" Mother reached for the
phone. "So long as you haven't had a fight,
I'm calling Ceegee. He can't jump to the
conclusion *I'm* coming on to him."

Steve was at Ceegee's house, so it ended
with both of them at our dinner table. The
talk was principally about the basketball
tournament, and my silence passed unnoticed.
Mother gave out seconds of apple upside-
down cake with whipped cream, and I began
to wonder whether our guests were ever
going home. I wasn't sure whether I wanted
them to go, or stay.

At last Dad looked pointedly at the old

schoolhouse clock, and they dragged themselves reluctantly to their feet. Dad let them out, locked up after them, and turned to regard me quizzically.

"I smell a consultation brewing. Your office or mine?"

"Mine." I led the way upstairs, and Dad followed.

"What's up?" he inquired. "You're not about to tell me you're quitting, are you?"

"Is anyone else in the high school computerizing the data you've given me?"

Dad's smile vanished. "What makes you think that?"

"I'd better show you." I took out the disks I'd brought home, booted up the computer, and retrieved the coded file. Behind me, I felt Dad stiffen.

"Where did you get this stuff from?" His voice was sharp.

"From the Gemini in the school computer lab. It had to have been in the machine's memory, from work somebody did on it after my class."

"You're sure you didn't get it off a system disk? You couldn't have taken one of mine to school by accident?"

"I know I didn't. Dad, can you read that language?"

"I can read those formulas," Dad retorted grimly. "That's what tipped you off, wasn't it?"

I nodded. "And there are a few others

here I haven't even passed on to you yet."

He scooped up the telephone and punched numbers with computer speed. The phone was answered quickly. Dad did not waste time on salutations.

"I'm at home. Come over right away, and bring everything you've got. That's right, everything. I'll explain when you get here." He pressed the disconnect button, hesitated, then dropped the phone in its cradle and was off for the stairs with me pelting after.

When I reached his study Dad was holding his phone book open with one hand and putting a call through with the other. "Web here. Can you come over? Yes, right now, to the house. Something's happened. I think you ought to know."

In the background I heard Mother moving around, filling the coffeepot. She was an old hand at emergency meetings.

Dad hung up. "We'd better meet in your digs, since the computer's there."

"Do you — want me in on it?" I asked awkwardly.

"You *are* in on it. Come on, I want to get another look at that mishmash before they get here." Dad did not explain who "they" were, and I didn't ask. We stared at the monitor, side by side, and the cryptic lines of type glowed at us inscrutably.

Distantly, a door opened. Mother's voice sounded, and another voice, vaguely familiar. A tall, thin man in his early thirties came up the stairs, halted in astonishment when he saw me.

"Hello, Mr. Jorgensen," I said quietly, masking my own surprise. He was a science teacher from the high school, a gaunt, handsome man with dark burning eyes.

"You know Sidney's been doing the computer filing and experimenting for me." Dad stated. "She's uncovered something important. Look." He pointed to the monitor. Thor Jorgensen drew his breath in a sharp whistle.

"Where did you get that from?" he demanded.

"I didn't. Sidney did. Off the internal memory of the Gemini."

"*What?*"

I repeated my story. "Do you know what that thing's saying?" I asked when I finished.

"All too well. I wrote it," Mr. Jorgensen answered grimly. "*Not* on the Gemini. I work on the computer in the science office, which does not have the off-power memory feature of the Gemini. I buy time on the school's mainframe, but no one could get at it without the proper code."

I did not mention what all the students knew — that hackers had been invading that mainframe for some time. I could tell from Dad's expression that he was rapidly losing any naivete he'd still had left. Mr. Jorgensen swung around. "Have you told Monahan?"

"He's on his way over. We'll have to let him in on all of it now." Dad scratched his head, grinning wryly at me. "By now you've deduced that Thor is my associate in Project Aardvark."

"Why couldn't you have told me?"

"Because, my dear child, on the one hand Project Aardvark is just too hot for any more people than necessary to be endangered by the knowledge of who and what's involved. On the other hand it's such a far-out idea, scientifically speaking, that neither of us can afford to jeopardize our credibility until we have concrete proof of alpha communication."

"Only somebody," Thor Jorgensen said very quietly, "doesn't seem to be concerned with waiting for that proof."

Dr. Webster didn't answer. I shuddered.

Monahan arrived. His eyebrows did not shoot up at the sight of either me or Jorgensen. "Thought there was more than recipes involved," he said casually, and squinted at the screen. "Anybody here make any sense of this?"

"*I* can," Jorgensen answered. "It's partly in a new computer language that isn't in much currency as yet." He mentioned the name, and Monahan nodded, grunting. "Part of what you see is my own code, in Danish; part is known physics and chemical formulas, and part is the result of our own research in —"

Monahan held up his hand. "Don't tell me. I probably wouldn't understand, and I'm probably better off not knowing. What I do understand is that somebody must have got this off the high school mainframe. How did you find out?"

Once again, I went through the explanations.

Monahan grunted again. Then, with a muttered, "May I?" he seated himself before the monitor and began scrolling through the entire six pages. When he had finished he swiveled around, his lower lip outthrust. "Whoever did this was tapping the school mainframe. Had to be. Probably networking somewhere else as well. The Gemini's good, but it's not that good."

I made a slight involuntary movement, which Monahan saw. His eyes narrowed. "What the hell's going on that I don't know about?" he demanded with deceptive quiet.

The others exchanged glances. Dad gave a wry, unamused smile. "Hang onto your chair, Hank. You're about to lose your protective innocence. And don't bother pretending you're just a dumb jock who can't understand. Your lab didn't get the testing of the Gemini just because you're an old football buddy of the inventor's dad."

"Don't tell me you were," Monahan said sardonically. He was stalling for time; I could see the wheels going around behind the steely eyes.

"Not Web. Me," Jorgensen said quietly. He was Monahan's junior in years and school seniority, but he seemed at that moment to grow in stature and authority. "I was in — school with the inventor . . . I'm afraid I can't say where."

"Classified," Monahan said, not moving. "I knew the guy was in government employment. I could — but I won't — take an educated guess which branch it was." Jorgensen looked relieved, but I felt another cold chill.

"We got worried, both of us," Mr. Jorgensen said simply. "About the end result of brain wave research in the hands of governments — any governments. That's why we both got out of that line of work. Government work, I mean. We each kept up with our own research. He's into high tech circuitry; me —" A faint smile curved his lips. "I guess I am, too, in a way. The circuitry of the human brain. I met Web while my wife was in the hospital, and we discovered our minds were working in the same direction."

Monahan just sat there like a buddha and chewed his cud. "You getting scared somebody might beat you to results?" he asked at last. "What the hell results are you after, anyway?"

Again, there was an exchange of glances. "Communicating with a computer via brain waves," Dad said. "Communicating *to* the human brain via computer. Ultimately, perhaps, the power to control brain waves via one."

Monahan was famous for never seeming surprised by anything. He achieved that now.

"Let me get this straight. Are you telling me that pile of chips sitting in my classroom can be operated by some kind of ESP?"

"We hope so, Hank," Dad said mildly. "That's what Sidney here is trying to find out."

Monahan squinted at me. "Any luck?"

"I was close, but — someone interrupted."

"And someone just happened to have pulled some of these geniuses' formulas into the Gemini's memory. You'd been programming similar material on the machine?"

"Yes, but not that. I hadn't gotten to that part of Dad's notes yet. And they were never out of my hands," I added quickly.

"What's on this screen right now," Mr. Jorgensen said flatly, "is material I haven't even turned over to Web yet."

"But you've worked on it. On a mainframe." It was not a question. Monahan heaved himself to his feet, and all at once the false serenity of the room was shattered. "Come on!"

"Where?" I blurted, as we stampeded down the stairs.

Monahan, already out the door, called back his answer in disgust, "School, of course! Hackers generally leave some traces!"

Monahan, being an athletics coach, had a key that unlocked the school's outer doors. That enabled us to avoid the notice of the custodians. Only night lights burned, and the school corridors were cold and eerie. Monahan unlocked the computer lab.

"Not yet!" Mr. Jorgensen said sharply as the coach's hand moved toward the light switch. He darted to the window and snapped down the blinds. Then he nodded, and the lights went on.

The computers in their neat rows crouched waiting like silent robots. Monahan turned to me. "Show me what you did."

I felt a strange sense of *déjà vu* as I sat down at the familiar work station and booted up the machine. I flicked on the tensor lamp. "The other lights were out," I murmured, and Dad moved to make the change. The Gemini and I were back again in that small, spellbound pool of light.

What keys had I touched then? My fingers hovered. Then, deliberately willing my mind to recreate the earlier actions, I called up all the data stored on both data and system disks. The copy I had made from the computer's memory flashed up brightly. The original version — the one stored in the computer itself — was nowhere to be found.

"How did you get it before?" Monahan demanded.

"I don't know! The intercom buzzed, and I — jumped. I don't know *what* I hit."

Monahan grunted and motioned for me to shift over. I did so. He hunkered down on the nearest chair, squinted, and began to rap out keyboard variations, his pudgy fingers traveling with surprising speed. At last he pushed away from the machine and leaned back heavily.

"Memory's been wiped clean."

My mouth felt dry. "You mean — somebody came back and erased that material deliberately?"

"Maybe. Maybe someone used the machine later, replacing that earlier machine-stored data with his own stuff. The machine only holds eight or ten K or so. At least, I assume it still does?" Monahan glanced at Jorgensen, who nodded. "So if somebody fed that much or more into the machine after Sidney left, it would replace the other."

"Only there's nothing in there as replacement," Dr. Webster pointed out, very quietly. Monahan shrugged.

"Doesn't have to mean anything. An operator using a shared machine generally would erase his material from computer memory, either as a courtesy or to preserve his privacy." He swiveled around. "I can tell you one thing, though. Nobody but Sidney had permission to use this machine after her class was over today. No students have permission to use this particular machine at all, except for her and the Rivington kid. And he couldn't have been in. He got out of school right after class to attend that three-hour computer lab session at the university."

I gave an involuntary exclamation. Then I stopped, as three male faces turned toward me. I wet my lips. "Nothing — I was just . . . staring at the screen."

I was staring at the monitor, but it was not the endless lines of gibberish that I saw. It was Josh, standing in the deserted hallway with his back to me, fifteen minutes before his lab class would have ended on a university campus a good half hour's walk away.

I didn't say it. I couldn't have said anything to save my soul.

Chapter 7

The Gemini was thoroughly examined, then shut down. Methodically, Monahan and Jorgensen went over the rest of the computer lab. They worked deftly, silently, communicating only in terse murmurs — two experienced searchers who knew exactly what they were looking for. Dad pulled out a chair and sat down, smiling faintly.

"Looks like the faculty is aware of a lot more hacking going on than the taxpayers of this fair city realize."

I hugged myself, feeling colder than the cold building warranted. At last the two teachers drew chairs up also, looking tired.

"Either nobody's been in here since I closed up the joint," Monahan said, "or whoever it was is sophisticated enough to leave no signs. Usually these kids get careless."

"Kids." Dad made the monosyllable half question, half a statement. Mr. Jorgensen shot him a sharp glance. Monahan pulled himself up again.

"Going to check the mainframe and networking records." He disappeared; came back looking sour. "Somebody's been freeloading on the school's time-share without signing for it again. The time tally's way too high for the accounted-for school use. Don't rule out kids, though. We've been having this problem ever since the lab first opened last fall. The computer jocks pride themselves on being able to break into any system."

I remembered, sickly, all the bragging that I'd heard. Monahan looked at Jorgensen. "What were you doing your work on? The file you rent in the school frame? The hospital mainframe?"

"Both."

"Looks like your secret password's not a secret anymore. Maybe you'd better tell your inventor pal to provide this baby with a fingerprint system as an ID method." Monahan shook himself. "We might as well close up. There's nothing more to find out here."

We left, after making a back-up copy of the gibberish disk and then carefully deleting *everything* that was in the Gemini's twenty-four hour memory.

I did not get much sleep that night.

Two out-of-the-ordinary things happened to me in school the next day. There was a locker search, and Joshua J. Rivington III was nice to me in class.

The locker search took place during a class

session in the morning. These occur a couple of times a year, whenever contraband substances on school premises are suspected. There's been some discussion of the legality of such searches, but so far the school board has always won on the grounds that the lockers and the locks themselves are school (i.e., town) property, merely loaned to the students. There were the usual sounds of indignation when we emerged from classes to find the search, by administration and selected faculty, in progress. It took a few minutes for the realization to penetrate my sleep-fogged brain. This wasn't a search for cherry bombs. It was a hunt by Jorgensen and Monahan for evidence of hacking related to Project Aardvark. If anything turned up, I was not told.

My experience with Rivington took me even more by surprise. It seemed an eon ago that barriers had come down when we laughed together. What I kept seeing — what I could not keep from seeing, though I would have died before I told — was Rivington in the hall outside the computer lab yesterday afternoon. Rivington all too available and capable of breaking into any data bank whatsoever.

I was at the Gemini, doggedly keyboarding away at Mother's recipes, when Josh walked in. He scanned the screen over my shoulder.

"1 C. bitter chocolate, grated. 1 tsp. vanilla. 1. C. grated coconut. Your mother's cookbook, I presume. It sounds good, what is it?"

I didn't look up. "The class assignment's done. Don't bother me."

"How'd you get the assignment?"

"Your method. Don't interrupt; I'm concentrating. *Drat!*" My finger struck the wrong key, and a gremlin ate the list of measurements.

Josh didn't say a word, but I sensed something being slid along the work station shelf beside the keyboard. It was a small object, wrapped in silver foil.

"Mocha truffles with toasted almonds. My creation," Josh said modestly. "Return favor for the sandwich yesterday."

"You didn't have to."

"I don't do things because I have to. And you don't usually act like this."

"I'm not acting like anything," I retorted, all to conscious that *acting* was the operative word.

"Yes you are. Like you're in a blue funk and mad at the world. That's my routine, not yours." Josh pulled up a chair. "Look, Webster, is anything wrong?"

"Oh, just let me alone, will you?" I exclaimed pettishly.

"Hey, children, ease up, can't you?" Ceegee had sloped over and was regarding us with a puzzled frown. Unfortunately his presence called up as many uncomfortable suspicions in me as did Josh's.

"What's got into you guys today?" he inquired, glancing from one of us to the other.

"Just tired," I said. Ceegee settled against

the Gemini, prepared to debate the point. Josh drew himself up.

"Do you mind, Richardson? This is a family fight."

"Oh. A fight, huh?" Ceegee thought the matter over and reluctantly backed off.

"We're not fighting," I said gruffly.

"Aren't we? That's a pleasant change." Josh waited a minute, then went on in a voice that was for him remarkably gentle. "Webster, is anything wrong?"

I didn't answer and after another minute he said matter-of-factly, "Okay, don't talk. I will. Are you doing anything this Saturday?"

"Why?"

"I thought I could give you some fencing lessons. In exchange for the programming you did for me yesterday."

"I told you you didn't have to pay me."

"And I told you, I don't do things I don't want to do. It isn't pay. I thought it could be fun. What do you say?"

"I don't know. I just don't know." That, at least, was the rock-bottom truth.

I didn't feel like facing the computer lab that afternoon. I started home instead, and Ceegee was lying in wait for me. "You don't look in any shape to be carrying valuable things like textbooks. Don't bother running off. You haven't the energy, and anyway, you need me."

"To carry my books?"

"To make you laugh," Ceegee said calmly.

"You sure look like you could use it. What happened, did somebody steal your teddy bear?"

"Don't you patronize me, too."

"Perish the thought," Ceegee said fervently. "I was thinking more along the lines of taking in a movie tonight. There's an old Laurel and Hardy film on cable."

"Gee, and here I thought you were asking me for a real date." The teasing tone rose to my lips automatically. "If you didn't spend so much money on your high tech playthings, you could afford cable TV yourself, you know."

"And lose my best excuse, next to your ma's cooking, to get you to spend time with me? I would ask you to a movie at the mall if I thought you'd say yes, even if Steve and Cordelia didn't chaperone." Ceegee's tone was light, but there was a note in it that sent a warning to my befuddled brain. I batted my eyelashes and tried to turn the whole thing into a joke.

"I didn't know you cared!! You mean a girl has a chance against computer chips, basketball, and cable, after all?"

"*You* would. Anyway," Ceegee said, elaborately nonchalant, "basketball will be over after the tournament. Maybe I'll take a shot then at sweeping you off your feet. Anyway, tonight may be the last time I'll have to cadge an invite to watch your cable stations for a while. I've got a good deal cooking."

To Ceegee's mind, a "good deal" could

mean only a computing job. All the remarks made last night about school hackers, and the devastating results of computer theft and fishing expeditions went whirling through my brain. My mouth felt dry.

"I guess I could put up with your company tonight, so long as Laurel and Hardy will be there, too. What is this deal that's cooking, anyway?"

"Just a deal," Ceegee said vaguely. "Something I ran across while hacking." We reached the boundary line of our respective homes and he handed me back my property. "In deference to the fact that I'll probably raid your refrigerator some time this evening, I won't do so now. See you later."

He was gone, leaving me standing in a snowdrift, feeling decidedly uneasy.

Laurel and Hardy lived up to their reputations. That was just as well, for it kept Ceegee engrossed in action on the screen instead of attempting another sort of action on the couch. My parents were out for the evening, and I had an uneasy feeling Ceegee was affectionately inclined. It was a delicate situation, but fortunately I didn't have to deal with it till the film was over. Then I evaded his encircling arm and made for the kitchen, with Ceegee more in pursuit of the Linzertorte than of me.

"If you ever get that cookbook of your mother's done, I'm going to make my mom buy a copy," Ceegee said through a very full mouth.

"What do you mean, 'if'? . . . Ceegee, what's this deal you were talking about this afternoon? Did you really get onto it by hacking?"

"Uh-huh. Can I have another piece of this? It's great."

I supplied it. "I guess you . . . get into a lot of things through hacking, don't you?"

Ceegee nodded. "Everybody does."

"You do, especially. You have a — I don't know — a real talent for cracking codes and things." I was sounding like the kind of girl that I despised — flirtatious, coy. I half expected Ceegee to gag. To my astonishment and dismay, he lapped it up.

"I guess I do. Steve's good, too, but he can't —" Ceegee started to laugh, scattering crumbs. "Did I ever tell you about the time he was trying to get into the SAT records and got into the government Social Security files instead?"

"He didn't!"

"Swear to God. He got out fast, before he did any harm. But he couldn't figure out how to get into them again later. Yours truly did. I didn't mess around any," Ceegee added virtuously. "I just checked out for my dad how much Social Security credit he had piled up. Not that he was grateful. He read me the riot act in six different positions, and then he called the Social Security office and checked my data, just to make sure I hadn't loused anything up."

"Did they find out?"

Ceegee was outraged. "My father is not a fink! And I am not an amateur. When I go into other people's files, I don't mess around or leave dirty messages for them to find." He came up behind me and slid an arm around my waist. "Look, do we have to talk about computers all the time?"

"I hear my parents coming," I murmured, ducking. There really was a car in the driveway. Soon there were two more Websters sitting at the kitchen table, drinking coffee. There was no more talk about computers, and there were no more passes made.

After Ceegee left I went upstairs, undressed, and went to bed. Some time later I heard my mother's footsteps on the stairs.

I lay there, staring at the ceiling and seeing in my mind's eye the strange code that was Project Aardvark. After a moment, before I could change my mind, I slid out of bed and into a robe and went downstairs to my father's study. He was stretched out in his recliner, puffing on his pipe. "Can't sleep?"

"No. Dad, there's something I — I'm afraid you have to know about." I recounted Ceegee's story of the jocks' forays into classified hacking. Dad listened without interruption.

"I don't think you have to worry what you're worrying," he said at last. "I can picture those two fudging with their SAT's, but

I really don't think Project Aardvark is their kind of thing. Or that they know enough about physics to tamper with it without making big mistakes." He reached out a hand, and I took it.

I felt bad about tattling, and I didn't feel any better after Dad's calm reaction. Because there were things I knew that he did not. One was that the jocks did computing and hacking for the sheer joy of the thing itself. It had nothing to do with the subject matter. Two was that they were good enough at programming and filing to do it accurately, without understanding one thing about the data they were working with. Three was that Ceegee had a photographic mind. Four was that if somebody was simply tapping into Dad's or Mr. Jorgensen's computer work and transmitting it, they could do that without doing any more than pushing a few buttons. They didn't have to mess around in the material itself.

I went back to bed, but I did not sleep. That was why, more than an hour later, I was able to scoop up the telephone on its first ring, so it would not wake my father who had an early call at the hospital.

"Dr. Webster's residence," I said guardedly, as we always do for late night calls.

The voice I heard almost made me drop the receiver.

"Sidney?" It was Josh, a Josh sounding odd and urgent. "I know it's late, but can I come over? I have to talk to you."

Chapter 8

Before he got there I had time to pull on slacks and a sweater and build up the kitchen fire. I watched for Josh's arrival, and let him in before he had a chance to ring the bell. He stood in the hall, his elegant coat dripping on the hooked rug.

"What did you want?" I asked baldly.

"We have to talk." Josh shifted his weight. "Look, I gather you're sore at me for some reason, but would it kill you to ask me to sit down? I can eat crow much better when I'm not so cold."

He did look cold and out of breath, as though he'd run most of the way over. I led the way into the kitchen and he followed, taking off his coat and folding it carefully across a chair. His eyes strayed to the Linzertorte sitting on the table. I turned the gas on under the tea kettle, produced cups and plates, and cut pieces of cake. "You were planning to eat some crow," I said pointedly, pushing the cake plate toward him.

Josh's mouth twisted. "What's with you, Webster? I thought the other day we were starting to get along. Now you're in a funk again. Can't you ever meet anybody half way?"

"I didn't know this was a summit meeting." The kettle boiled and I made hot chocolate in Mother's prized Japanese chocolate pot. I was showing off, and I knew it. I also knew Josh appreciated it. We looked at each other, then away.

"If this isn't going to be a breakfast conference," I said carefully, "you'd better get around to explaining what you want."

"I want you to come back to work. For real. Not beginner's stuff." Josh took a gulp of cocoa and looked at me directly. "You were right, what you said. I was hogging the good stuff. I hate not doing everything myself. But I can't. I took on too much, the clients are driving me crazy. And some of the work I — just don't have a handle on. There, if that's not eating crow, I don't know what is."

Coming from Josh, that was a magnificent apology. Also flattering. And my emotions and intentions were going back and forth like a Ping-Pong ball.

"I don't think I should," I said at last. "We do — get on each other's nerves."

"Not always." A faint smile tugged at his mouth, and I knew he was remembering the other day in the lab.

I persevered. "If people don't work together well, it messes up the work. You know that. You and I both want to be boss. And besides, I really do have a lot of work already."

"The cookbook?" Josh asked, watching me closely. "Bull."

"What?"

"You heard me. You wouldn't get as close-mouthed and uptight as you're getting, and quit a job you'd taken on, just for a cookbook your mother may or may not actually publish. Other people might, but not you." He put his hands up, as I opened my mouth to explode. "I'm not knocking cookbooks! I'm just saying you're acting as if you're working on something more urgent. Or serious. Or both."

So he *could* notice things about people, after all. "You're right," I said at last, slowly. "I am working on something else, too. A research project for — someone my father knows." That ought to cover things if whoever was stealing the Project Aardvark material knew it was Dad's. "I'm not just being stubborn. I really don't see how I can spread myself any thinner, and still do justice to everything."

"At least look at the work before you decide." Josh wasn't giving up easily. He opened the attaché case and took out two folders. "Both of these are scientific — or supposed to be. The first one you know about, the pharmaceutical firm. The other's for an independent scientist in California, and it's far out."

He spread the work specifications out enticingly. The pharmaceutical project *was* interesting, even giving my loathing of chemistry. I could see fascinating opportunities for creative computing, and they were exactly the sort of things for which I suspected Josh lacked imagination.

"I really don't think I'd better," I started to say with genuine regret. And then I looked at the second folder, and for a moment my heart may have stopped.

"Real world-of-tomorrow stuff," Josh said, "isn't it? Guy's trying to develop a method of communicating with a computer by ESP. Mental telepathy, can you believe it?"

"You ... don't think it can be done," I said, dry-lipped.

"I think *computers* can be made to emit messages by energy waves. Whether humans can is something else." Josh shrugged. "It's his money. If he wants to throw it away devising experiments, I'll do the programming."

"How is this communication supposed to take place?"

Josh looked puzzled. "I think he'd settle for Morse code, or graphics symbols like on the cards used to test for ESP, or anything he could get. The best bet would probably be some sort of contact pad to respond to body rhythms, something like lie detectors use." He snickered. "Kids' Christmas toy of the future, I suppose. Draw your own 3-D cartoons by *thinking* the pictures into place!"

He didn't say anything about altered states of consciousness. He didn't say anything about serious medical, military, or other use. I breathed again.

It was perfectly possible for more than one researcher to be working on mental communication with a computer at the same time. Scientists had been trying to prove or disprove mental telepathy for centuries, and computers were the current inventors' gold mine. All the same, it would be good to find out all I could about what this mad scientist in California was up to.

I said, as though I were deliberating a work schedule, "This pharmaceutical project is intriguing. I suppose maybe I could squeeze it in. So long as it didn't take me away from the work I'm already doing, of course."

"Of course." Josh looked as though he'd settle for anything I could give him. He must really be up a tree where work flow and deadlines were concerned. "What is this other job that's so important?"

I fished out my Mona Lisa smile. "I'm afraid I can't say. You know how business firms are about secrecy. Protecting patents, and things." That should, I hope, have strewn enough red herrings to throw him off the track.

"Oh. Sure," Josh said without rancor. "Actually, this stuff's pretty top secret, too. I had to sign secrecy agreements. I'd better make some up for you to sign, too. I couldn't have shown you these papers if you hadn't been working with me on the projects."

So he'd taken for granted I would come back to work. Or else he'd taken a big chance, and I didn't think he was a gambler. "My father's my agent," I said grandly. "He'll draw up papers."

We parted in an atmosphere of mutual cordiality.

"I certainly will draw up papers," Dad said in the morning when he heard my report. "Papers that will make sure you can't be accused of passing on information, if the ESP project turns out to be anything close to mine. How much did you tell Josh about Project Aardvark?"

"*Nothing!* I only said I was working on a research project for a business firm, something that was going to be patented."

"Good. Don't say anything else. And don't let Josh see if anything strikes you as peculiar. Just come tell me."

"Dad, you don't think Josh is the one —"

"I'm trying not to speculate, and confine myself to things I know. I *know* someone in Lakeland was, maybe still is, getting into our research."

Dad drew up a work-and-secrecy agreement right after breakfast. It was a masterpiece. When I showed it to Josh he raised his eyebrow and said he'd like to have my father draw up *his* contracts. But he signed, and so did I. "Okay," he said, completing the *J. J.*

Rivington III with a flourish. "Can we get started after school today?"

It was Friday, so I could work on Project Aardvark that night and through the weekend. "All right," I said.

This conversation took place in the cafeteria, where for once Josh had turned up and eaten lunch. We signed the contracts under Mr. Hazzard's benign eye and then talked him into passes to the computer lab.

We made a start on the pharmaceutical work during lunch period and continued during class. Monahan, passing by, took a look and told us we could hand some of it in for extra credit if we wished. After school I went straight to the lab without visiting my locker first, partly because I didn't plan to need the Project Aardvark material, and partly because I suspected Ceegee would be around the locker. Josh had not yet arrived.

I turned on the computer and then realized I could not boot it up, because there was no system disk available till Josh got there. Monahan locks up the school disks as soon as class is over. I glanced at the clock and decided I might as well run down and get mine; Ceegee would probably have given up by now. I'd started carting my books around in a canvas tote, it being easier to transport with the attaché, since both had handles. I left the tote bag next to the computer.

Luck wasn't with me. Ceegee was still around. Encouraged by my interest in his hacking, he wanted to take me to the movies

Saturday night. I retrieved the attaché case from my locker, making loud groans about how the cookbook stuff inside was going to keep me occupied all weekend. Then Monahan came by and told Ceegee to beat it to the gym for practice, and I escaped.

Josh was in the lab when I reached it, and had already booted up.

"Thought maybe you weren't going to show," he said.

"Went to get my system disk in case *you* didn't show," I retorted. "What are you working on?"

"I've loaded the pharmaceutical material in the Gemini memory. Why don't you go on with the multi-line graph you suggested, and I'll cross-file the next batch of data in another computer?"

That particular division of labor was a sound idea. "I think I have the format for the graph in my notebook somewhere," I said, remembering earlier doodling.

I reached without looking down into the canvas tote. Something smooth and tepid coiled itself around my wrist.

I screamed.

Josh got to me so fast he knocked a chair over in his speed. By the time my arm, and the snake clinging to it, was out of the tote bag, he was already pulling off the reptile.

We contemplated it warily as he held it, correctly, its neck between his forefinger and thumb. The other foot and a half, or more, of it thrashed in annoyance.

I took a deep breath. "Thanks."

"You wouldn't scream over nothing," Josh said grimly.

"It is nothing. That kind's harmless. Snakes give me the creeps, but I finally got over being afraid of them by the end of biology last year. Which is probably where this one came from, by the way — the science lab. At least one escapes, or is persuaded to escape, every year. They cause a big sensation when they turn up in lockers. One time it was the ventilating vent in the vice-principal's office." I was beginning to babble. "I'd better take him back to his cage."

"*We'll* take him back," Josh said firmly. So we all went, Josh and I and our attaché cases and the snake, who by this time had decided Josh was a tree he wished to climb. We had to get the new custodian to let us in to the science lab, and he thought our having the snake was very fishy. Josh made up some tale to tell him, and we finally got inside and put the snake back in his cage. Its top had been slightly ajar, which explained a lot.

"Somebody was careless," Josh commented.

"Speaking of careless, we left the computer on with your disks in it." We dashed back, but nothing had been tampered with. I checked the disks and the Gemini's memory while Josh wasn't looking, and nothing relating to Project Aardvark appeared.

We didn't get as much work done as we'd hoped, and I didn't tell my parents about the snake. Josh and I had decided to keep that to ourselves.

I worked on Project Aardvark at home that night. On Saturday morning, Ceegee called to repeat his movie invitation. I said no. Early Saturday afternoon Josh showed up, I thought for work, but what he had in mind was that fencing lesson. We went out in the driveway, borrowing handles from garden tools for the purpose, and ended up looking pretty silly, especially Josh with his coattails flapping in the breeze.

We were just getting pretty slap-happy, and the fencing was degenerating into a snowball fight, when a car pulled into the driveway next door. It contained most of the basketball team and Cordelia. Josh immediately got his dignity back again, and took his leave almost as soon as the gang piled over.

Ceegee was pursuing a movie date again. When I finally got through to him that the answer was no, he and the ball players departed, leaving Cordelia looking at me thoughtfully.

"You didn't have to be quite so mean, did you?"

"I wouldn't have, if he'd just take a hint! Or a straight *no* for an answer."

"Maybe he would if you gave it to him straight."

I looked at her, startled. "What am I supposed to do, tell him I love him like a brother? That's not what he wants to hear."

"Maybe he'd rather hear that than have

false hope." When I started to protest, she cut me off. "Last night, when the crowd went for pizza after the game, Ceegee was really *up*, because something you'd said to him the other night gave him the idea he had a chance with you after all. You should have been at the game. Ceegee scored fifty points. Even more than Steve."

"That's why I wasn't there, so he wouldn't get ideas. Anyway, I had work to do."

"Work!" Cordelia made it a dirty word. "It's not bad enough I have to listen to the jocks burble about computers? At least they're human enough to descend to just playing games on the darn things once in a while! You know what you're turning into lately? A — a preprogrammed, dehumanized robot like Rivington. I've heard of computer addiction, but I never thought it would hook Miss Empathize-with-Everyone!"

"That's a nasty thing to say!"

"Which? The robot part or the empathy part?" Cordelia demanded bluntly. "I've got empathy, too, you know, enough to believe you don't really realize you're turning into a first-class witch. In case you weren't tuned in enough to notice, you *did* turn Ceegee on the other night. Maybe you think that's funny, but he didn't."

I couldn't tell her I'd done it, not for fun and games, but to find out whether Ceegee had been stealing my father's work. I went into the house wishing I'd never heard of Project Aardvark.

Chapter 9

I spent a miserable Sunday, getting some but not much done on my various projects, and on Monday in school I was hailed for a private heart-to-heart with Monahan.

"Any more mumbo-jumbo show up on the SMN?" That was Monahan's facetious way of referring to Project Aardvark.

"Not yet."

Monahan grunted. "I hear our string bean friend has been using his smarts to get into government files. Think he's using them anywhere else he oughtn't?"

So Dad had passed on the results of my playing Mata Hari. "I don't know," I answered guardedly.

"And would rather not, huh? Can't say I blame you. Never mind," Monahan said heavily, and patted me on the shoulder. "I'll follow up on it. You won't have to get involved."

The shoulder pat infuriated me. There was no use telling me to stay home with my dolls like a good little girl. I was a part of Project Aardvark, and it was perfectly disgusting to find myself wishing that I wasn't.

I didn't have to force myself in any direction where Ceegee was concerned that day. During lunch period he was wrapped up in a basketball strategy discussion with the other jocks, and he removed himself from computer class by presenting Monahan with a completed assignment and a request for a pass to the gym. Monahan obliged. Josh showed up in class late, in a foul mood, and didn't accomplish much more than I did myself.

The truth was, I was just too tired to think. I'd had a week of very little sleep and uncomfortable suspicions, and my stomach was acting like it used to when I had to dance a solo in a recital. Except that Project Aardvark was so very much more important, and I was better at computing than I'd ever been at dancing. So why was I feeling exactly like that long-ago, in-over-her-head little girl? I was a fine one, wasn't I, to feel one up on Josh for biting off more than he could chew?

Nobody was hanging around for me when school got out. Even Josh did not turn up in the computer lab, having business of some kind at the university. "At least that SMN still loves me. Or is learning to. I hope," I told myself. How I felt about that computer at that moment was, to say the least, equivocal.

Monahan, who'd been waiting for me to show up, was chafing at the bit. "She's all yours this afternoon, so you'll have to make sure everything is closed up properly. I'll lock the classroom door as I go out. You'll be able to turn the bolt in the door so you can leave, but no one can get in without a key. I've told the custodians not to come in if they see you here, so you won't have to worry if you're working on classified material."

"Mr. Hazzard?"

Monahan's mouth twisted. "He's already left. His wife had some kind of crisis, so she pulled him out of practice. *I* have to get to the gym to take over before the baboons go ape." He pulled out his thick ring of keys, locked the door as he said he would, and left.

Being alone in here was beginning to take on all the aspects of a recurring dream, with the snake motif thrown in for a macabre touch. What should I work on first? I booted up, took out the Project Aardvark material, and contemplated the mystery printout with a kind of baffled desperation. It was as indecipherable as something out of the Dark Ages, even after my initiation into Josh's pharmaceutical formulas. What I needed, I thought, was a touchstone like the Dark Ages alchemists had sought to tell true gold from dross.

My fingers tapped the letters into the SMN III's keyboard. T - O - U - C - H - S - T - O - N - E.

The monitor screen glowed with light.

I stared at it until it swam, then closed my eyes. Project Aardvark. What had gotten me into it, anyway? What had gotten DAD into it? Helping people. The unknown.

Danger? The word flashed into my mind from nowhere. Danger. Surgeons lived with danger, and with challenge. Risk was their shadowy companion. Even the risk that whatever they most knew, most surely believed, could at any moment be proved wrong. Dad, the rationalist, embarking on something as irrational as the notion of communicating with machinery by brain waves. . . .

My thoughts stopped coming in logical word patterns, and started coming, as they often did when I was tired, in pictures. Funny, how many people never thought in pictures. Once, when I was little, I'd said something about those pictures in my head to Ceegee, and he'd looked at me as if I'd come from outer space. Maybe now that he pumped so much money into videogames with graphics, he'd no longer find that strange.

He probably thought I was pretty strange right now, anyway.

Cordelia said I was getting witchy. Meaning insensitive. Meaning uncaring. Meaning hard. The swift picture of Cordelia shouting at me rose, and was replaced by another. Ceegee, expanding under the sun of my calculated interest, that night we'd watched TV. Ceegee telling me how he'd gotten into Social Security Administration records, thinking there was nothing wrong with that, since he hadn't altered anything, just copied out some data. Being proud of it, thinking it was an accomplishment, harmless fun. Lots of people considered the data in mainframe computers public domain, not private property. Theirs for the taking.

Steve Wiczniewski thought so, too, didn't he? Steve got into the Social Security files first. Cordelia, who in all else was so ethical it hurt, was secretly proud of Steve's fiendish ingenuity. Pictures were diamond-bright behind my eyes. . . . Cordelia in the cafeteria, Cordelia by the swimming pool, Cordelia in my office, laughing with delight over Steve's exploits.

And Josh the computer genius, who was hired to work on an ESP communication project. Josh attending advanced university courses while still in high school. Heaven only knew what Josh was capable of, if he put his mind to something totally.

Joshua J. Rivington III + SMN III = X.

I saw a dozen Joshes; in the cafeteria, in the hall, the classroom. In the computer store downtown, peeling off thousands of dollars' worth of bills. And other images I had seen only in my mind. . . Josh at the SMN Gemini, keying into a mainframe somewhere, summoning or keying in the Project Aardvark symbols. . . .

The pictures were so vivid I almost cried out in pain.

What are you really up to, Joshua J. Rivington III? What are you doing with my

SMN that I don't know? And you, SMN, darn you, why aren't you living up to your advance billing? Cordelia says I'm a witch. You're the one who's being a witch. You're maddening, tantalizing, aloof. Addictive! Like an adventuress that's never really knowable, despite the promise! SMN . . . Samantha . . . that's what I'll call you, since I have to call you *something*. You're the only one who knows what Josh is up to. Why won't you be the touchstone you're supposed to be? Darn you, HELP me!

My fingers tingled. I felt as if everything were shifting to slow motion. Colors flowed before my eyes, like the shifting veils of color on that sixty-inch screen in the New York art gallery I visited once with Dad. A screen that had been computer-linked to a stereo and was showing Bach's *Airs for a D String* transformed into moving shapes of light. I was there in the darkened classroom, watching the memory of this with my eyes closed. I was somewhere removed and above, watching myself watching. I was very calm. The room sang with silence.

I opened my eyes and was looking straight at the monitor's luminous screen.

H O W   C A N   I   H E L P   Y O U?

The shimmering letters burned before my eyes and in my brain. It was several moments before they formed themselves into words in my dreamily relaxed awareness.

I had established alpha contact with the SMN III at last.

Chapter 10

I had made contact, and the computer was responding to me with a question. The piece of my mind that was standing apart, watching, automatically dictated the proper step-by-step programming techniques. But Sidney Scott Webster's unconscious ran the show. I felt as I used to, long ago, sleigh-riding alone down a hill onto the frozen lake in twilight.

I was aware of all this vaguely, as if it was being stored into some mental data bank for future reference. What was real were the thoughts flashing full-blown into my mind, and the answers flashing onto Samantha's screen.

What is Josh doing?

DOES NOT COMPUTE.

I summoned a mental image of the gibberish I'd found on Samantha's screen. *Who computed this?*

UNKNOWN.

Where did it come from?

S A C A M, Samantha glibly flashed back. It could be the name of a data bank, but it was unknown to me.

At least we know the hacker wasn't poaching Dad's or Mr. Jorgensen's files, I responded automatically.

D A D , J O R G E N S E N , D O N O T C O M P U T E, Samantha agreed.

There's a lot you don't know yet, isn't there? I thought wrathfully. *And not enough time. Darn it, Samantha, why did you take this long to talk to me?*

C A N N O T R E T R I E V E W H A T I S N O T F I L E D, Samantha retorted smugly. D A R N D O E S N O T C O M -P U T E.

It does now.

Somebody banged on the door. My pulses jumped, and the screen went blank.

The custodian, Wiggins, was visible through the door's glass window, gesturing firmly. I walked groggily over.

"I know Monahan said let you alone, but I gotta get in there. It's five-thirty, see?"

"Okay." I opened the door. The alpha contact was broken, and I knew in my bones it could not be reestablished. That is, not now. But it would be again, sometime soon.

It was not until I was halfway home that I realized I had no tangible evidence of what had occurred. Storing the "conversation," or printing out a copy, had not crossed either my conscious, or unconscious mind.

* * *

It was nearly nine p.m. before Dad got home and I was able to make a full report. He cut short my apology about no proof. "The SMN's internal memory may still have it . . . if nobody's monkeyed with it since." He punched numbers into the telephone, handed it to me, and started for the door. "Tell Monahan to meet us at the school. I'll go warm up the car."

Another late-night session at the school. Monahan was there already, at a late basketball practice. His wife could not get word to him because the school switchboard had closed at five. She telephoned Mr. Jorgensen for me, and he was waiting right inside the door from the parking lot when Dad and I arrived. A fat ring of keys dangled from his fingers.

"I guessed what you wanted and got these from Monahan. He's in the gym; he can't leave practice yet. What's up?"

"Eureka, I think, is the appropriate word. If we're lucky. Sidney wants to see if the SMN's internal memory's still retaining the last thing she'd called up on the screen."

We hurried to the computer lab. Mr. Jorgensen locked the door after us and taped a piece of paper across its clear glass pane. Dad started to reach for the light switch, but I stopped him.

"Don't, please. And stay here till I see what

I can do. People around make it hard to concentrate." I had some vague idea of reestablishing the earlier contact.

Samantha's on-screen memory had been cleared. If only there was some way I could crack into her "hidden menu." I stared at the blank screen helplessly.

"We can save time." Mr. Jorgensen turned on a nearby Apple and tossed me Monahan's key ring. "Find me a modem."

I obeyed silently. He rigged it rapidly to Monahan's desk telephone. "We can fight about this with the school bookkeeper afterwards," he murmured, keying code letters into the Apple at top speed. "I'm calling the Gemini's inventor. It's what, six-thirty in California now? He's probably still at his office."

Within minutes, an answer flashed. H E Y , G O O D   B U D D Y .   H O W ' S   P R O J - E C T   G O I N G ?

Jorgensen's fingers flew. T H R E A T - E N E D .   A D V I S E   H O W   R E A D I N T E R N A L   M E M O R Y .

C O N T R O L .   D A T E   W E   C A M E H O M E .   M Y   W I F E ' S   L O G O . The answer appeared on the screen.

"The guy wasn't in the Secret Forces for nothing," Jorgensen said happily, tapping in a swift T H A N K S ,   B U D D Y , and signed off. "I'll write this down for you afterwards," he told me, shifting over to Samantha to key in the date and initials so cryptically indicated.

The screen blinked twice, and my conversation with Samantha came into view.

"Samantha — that's what I call her — has it. So I didn't zap it when I shifted back to beta —" I started to say. The words died on my lips. Jorgensen had frozen; Dad literally shoved him aside, peered at the screen, and gave a low stunned whistle.

"SACAM."

Thor Jorgensen pushed back in his chair and nodded. "Don't know why we're so surprised. It figures, doesn't it?"

"What figures?" I demanded.

Jorgensen chose his words carefully. "A while ago, a college kid in California cracked into a top-secret information network. It had been set up for . . . mutual research and development use by the government, and the defense department, and companies that were developing projects for future consideration."

Projects like Dad's alpha work. The thought flashed instantly, and with it the memory of what Dad had said about the harm that could be done via alpha-wave-controlled computers. My mouth felt dry. "You mean the — the defense department may already have your research and be developing weapons applications?"

"Not necessarily," Dad said quickly. "But *somebody* has it. How they got it, and for what purpose, is up for grabs. But thanks to you and your friend here," he patted Samantha's side, "we now know our data's being fed into SACAM."

"All of it?" I demanded.

"We don't know that yet, do we?" Dad's voice was too casual, a sign that he was deeply troubled. He looked at Jorgensen, and the physics teacher spoke with decision.

"I can take a couple of personal days off. I'll fly to California and talk to Bud. I still have security clearance. I'll see the guys at SACAM and alert them to the fact that somebody's cracked in again. Something much bigger than just our own project here could be involved."

"Is SACAM the same network the college student cracked?" I asked. Jorgensen shook his head.

"That was closed down, and two new ones were set up. One strictly for contact with the government's own research and development programs. Another one for the use of the private sector and independent scientists who work with the government."

"SACAM."

Jorgensen nodded. "If someone's been messing with it, for fun or something worse, there's going to be hell to pay. A lot of valuable research data may have been damaged, and that's just the beginning."

I shivered.

Monahan arrived, was let in and brought up to date.

"Has that project of yours been harmed?" he asked the other men immediately.

"We won't know that till Thor gets to California, will we?" Dad's voice had that tone again. I could fairly see wheels going around in his head. "Neither of us has put any secret material on that network. I haven't even used it. Have you, Thor?"

"Not for anything but asking questions that were phrased too carefully to give anything away. I haven't stored any of our data on *anything* but my own disks."

"And Sidney's made sure the work she's been doing on this machine has been wiped out of everything except her own disks, which she's kept locked up." Dad glanced at the attaché case. "Someone's getting our data. I don't buy the explanation of simultaneous research results," he said, and I thought of Josh's crackpot scientist, and shivered. "There's too much that was ours alone in that code sheet the SMN coughed up earlier. The only conclusion I can come to is that somebody's getting into the hospital mainframe. I have used that, and it's supposed to be theft-proof. Or else someone's getting into our notes and disks."

Thor Jorgensen looked gray. "Mine have been locked up in the safe in my office here."

Because the office contained chemicals for experiments and also his own personal computer, it had a dead-bolt lock, and his safe had a combination only he knew. *Or was supposed to know*. The thought was in everybody's mind. "I even kept the stuff in a smelly old gym bag. Figured that would make it less attractive, if anybody did manage to come poking."

The school buzzer system signaled that it was ten-thirty. Night or day, the buzzers set for the various class periods went off on schedule. Monahan stirred. "Practice will be getting out. Some of those jokers will take this corridor to their cars, even if they're not supposed to. Saves them two minutes of walk out in the cold. What now?"

"Print a copy of Sidney's conversation with Samantha." Dad picked up the name I had given the SMN, and everybody grinned. "Then wipe out everything so nobody can read it later."

Somebody banged on the door, and the lock rattled.

As one, Dad and Jorgensen moved to shield the printer I was working at from view. Samantha's screen was invisible from the door because of the work center partition. Monahan strode over with a speed unexpected in so heavy-set a man, and pulled off the paper taped across the window. We heard him exclaim, "Hazzard?"

The gym teacher unlocked the door. "I saw the light through the smoked glass as I came by, and thought some kids were fooling around. Didn't know you were in here." He saw us over Monahan's shoulder, and frowned.

"It's okay. The kid left something behind today, so her dad brought her over for it. Jorgensen and I were here anyway, so I let them in." General introductions followed. Hazzard looked uninterested and anxious to get home. He asked Monahan perfunctorily, "Get those records done?"

"Yep. Thanks for taking over practice for me. I found there's been a mistake in the printouts of last marking period's grades for two of my classes. Gremlins must have gotten into the computer," Monahan explained blandly. "That's how you happened to find me here."

Dad took the cue. "We mustn't keep you any longer. Come along, Sidney. Nice meeting you, Hazzard."

At last we were out in the parking lot in the black night. A faint icy snow was falling. Jorgensen stood for a moment by Dad's car door. "I don't like this, Scott."

"Nor do I. And I think it's time I got Sidney *out* of it."

"*Dad!*" I looked from one pair of protective male eyes to the other and said firmly, "You *can't* take me off. I'm the only connecting link you have between Project Aardvark, Samantha, and the students. You'll need that, if it *is* students who've been hacking. And I can make alpha contact with Samantha. *You* can't. You both are trained to think scientifically all the time. It would take too long to learn to let go of beta consciousness. And we don't have time, do we?"

Jorgensen tactfully withdrew. Dad gunned the motor and we rode home in silence. Once in our own warm garage, with the door closed and locked, he turned to look at me thoughtfully.

"All right," he said at last, and there was an odd note in his voice. "I hate everything about this, but it *is* dangerous, and we *do* need you anyway. So you're still on the payroll. Under two conditions. Every night — or early morning, if I get home too late for you to stay awake — you are to report to me everything that happened the day before, however trivial, that could have any bearing on Samantha and the project. And you are not to have the Project Aardvark material with you at any time you could be vulnerable to attack."

I stared at him. "Dad, I've been carrying it around with me all the time! And there's always loads of people around, so nobody could try anything." My voice faltered.

"You're alone in the classroom at times. Free periods, and after school."

"Monahan showed me how to lock myself in when Josh isn't with me."

Dad still looked dissatisfied. "I'll arrange with Monahan about your using his desk phone. I want you to telephone home every time you lock yourself in there, to report how long you'll be there, and call again when you're ready to leave. If your mother's not home, call my answering service. And you're not to walk home with that attaché case. One of us will come to drive you home."

I could not deny the wave of relief that surged through me. It showed me how strong and how deep-buried my own fear had become. I said, in a more normal voice, "That would be great. But you won't have to provide chauffeur service every day. Lots of times I walk home with the other kids. They'd think it queer if I stopped. And they'll —"

My voice dwindled. *They'll take care of me*, I'd been about to say. Suddenly the words took on another, ominous meaning. Because if the phantom hacker was someone so familiar with Lakeland High School, it could be anyone connected with it. Even Steve Wiczniewski. Even Ceegee. Even Josh.

Chapter 11

On Tuesday I was in a fog, which had nothing whatever to do with alpha state or Samantha. I wished I could zap into an altered state of consciousness and escape what was constantly on my mind.

This is silly. I'm not accomplishing anything, just wasting time, I told myself. If I couldn't find out who was ripping off Dad's research, I could at least get some work done on it — or on Josh's projects. Having told myself this, I didn't sign out of cafeteria for the computer lab. I went to the school library instead, where nobody could talk to me, to collect my thoughts.

Once I applied myself, it didn't take Samantha to sort out the problems.

1. Project Aardvark was not going to succeed unless:
   a. The computer rip-offs and leaks were stopped.
   b. I concentrated hard enough to get the processing and the alpha state experiments completed.

2. I wasn't going to be able to concentrate until I stopped suspecting everyone I knew.
3. I couldn't stop those suspicions until the phantom hacker(s) were uncovered.
4. I wouldn't stop feeling — *equivocal*, I guess, summed it up best — about Josh and the work I was doing for him (especially the ESP material) until then, also.

Therefore: I had better apply myself to uncovering the hacker, before I became either manic-depressive or schizophrenic. Because as far as I could tell, *I* was the only real connecting link between Project Aardvark and the likely suspect, or the leads to them (meaning Josh). *Therefore*: I should shelve the visions of Sidney Scott Webster as superscientist or superprogrammer, and come to terms with Sidney Scott Webster, detective.

I didn't like any of this, but once faced, it couldn't be ignored. At least my thinking had become much clearer. So I went to Monahan's class, and my new resolutions dissolved before the sight of all my friends and suspects there together. Including Josh. Especially Josh. That's when it started striking me full-force how much I didn't want for him to be involved.

Cordelia had been right about Josh and me all along, hadn't she?

I fled from the thought into the work Josh had waiting for me, a Josh who was feeling very pleased with everything. "I got started on the program for the crackpot. See what you think."

There wasn't much traffic around Samantha, everyone being occupied elsewhere. I secluded myself and his printout behind my notebook, took a look, and got a huge shock.

Josh had about twenty very logical and very theoretic steps worked out for communicating with a computer via brain waves.

I looked at him over the top of the notebook. "You're assuming the computer exists that can handle this."

"The crackpot's assuming it." Josh was very noncommittal. "All we're doing is developing instructions to teach the computer how, step by step."

That "we" jabbed at a sore spot in my conscience. So did his offhand follow-up. "If you see any changes you think should be made, go ahead. See if you can go on with the instructions, anyway. I've run dry. I've got some notes to make."

Exactly how I was to write two separate brain wave communication programs, one for Project Aardvark and one for Josh, was one of those points of ethics I had so far avoided. I was going to have to talk to Dad about the evidence implicating Josh, whether I wanted to or not.

I stared at the printout until Josh, puzzled, inquired if I was okay. "Yes. Sorry. Look, you can use the Gemini all period, if you want. I have to think."

"Stuck?" Josh asked, amused.

"Sort of. I've run up against a . . . a couple of alternatives. I can't go on till I work them out."

Surprisingly, he did not argue. I withdrew with my notebook and my crisis, and Josh pounded away at Samantha as if he didn't have a worry on his brain.

Towards the end of the period a student came in with a summons from the principal, which Monahan scanned. "Wiczniewski, Richardson, Sommers. Mr. Tanner's office, on the double." They made their exits under cover of muttered witticisms. All were accomplished hackers. Had Monahan started the wheels turning to find out if one of them had been tapping into the school's data bank time-sharing? I shot him a look which Monahan returned impassively.

Ceegee had left his bulging notebook on the floor by his work station. Suddenly, I did not want Monahan to find it. I went to the shelves where the computer games were kept, selected one, and returned to my chair by way of Ceegee and Steve's station. As I reached for it, I let the game slip from my arms. When I picked it up, I gathered Ceegee's notebook into my arms as well.

The class bell rang.

That settled it; Ceegee would not be returning, because his last class was down on the first floor. I grabbed my own belongings and made my way to the nearest girls' room. As usual, it was jammed. If I wanted privacy I would have to cut my class.

Almost as if I'd been programmed against my will, I did so. I locked myself into the last cubicle, which had the advantage of two solid walls, and deliberately started to go through Ceegee's notebook. Twice I had to pick up debris and papers which fell out. After fifteen minutes, I admitted relieved defeat. There was nothing that connected Ceegee in any way with Project Aardvark. Unless —

My heart started pounding. Unless there was something I hadn't recognized among the cryptic list of alphabet-plus-number scribbles. They looked like code, like passwords. Hackers used passwords to crack into data banks, and somebody around here had cracked into SACAM.

Feeling like a traitor, I copied down the list.

By the time I was finished, the dismissal bell had rung. I had missed my whole last class. I went downstairs, heading for the lost and found to drop the notebook, and as luck would have it encountered Ceegee emerging from Mr. Tanner's office. I took a deep breath.

"You left this up in Monahan's room."

"Gee, thanks." Ceegee did not look troubled over either the notebook or the apparently not very serious interview with Mr. Tanner. He did not look uncomfortable about coming face to face with me, so maybe his crush was wearing off. It was I who looked uncomfortable, and I knew it. I handed him the notebook, wished him luck in the game that night, and departed with all possible speed.

Where I was heading I still had not decided. I reached the computer lab to find Josh in possession of Samantha and programming happily away. I did not go in. There was one thing I had to do, and I had to do it without an audience.

I went home, straight up to my office, and connected my computer to a modem. I had Dad's list of data bank and network telephone numbers; I had his credit number for using them; I had the list from Ceegee's notebook. I set up the computer to try every possible combination, and sat there reading the incriminating evidence as it rolled in.

When at last it was all captured on a printout, I was bone-tired and shaky, and my stomach couldn't make up its mind whether to be sick or not. Ceegee's hacking — or his collection of numbers for possible future hacking — was wide-ranging. I had reached everything from computer game networks to a geriatrics institute to multinational corporations. Along the way I'd plugged into government computers from the Department of the Navy to Social Security and the IRS.

But none of all those many tries had led to SACAM.

I closed down the computer and went downstairs, and everything there seemed so normal. Mother was throwing together one of her last-minute dinners — boneless chicken with mushrooms and tomatoes, and spaghetti. The smell was heavenly, but it made me feel queasy. I dropped down in one of the big chairs by the kitchen fire.

"Mom, when's Dad getting home?"

"He isn't. He had a two-day conference to go to, don't you remember? He won't be back till some time tomorrow evening."

"He didn't mention it."

Mother laughed and said Dad had probably forgotten it himself until his secretary reminded him, and I felt as if I'd had an eleventh-hour reprieve. I wouldn't have to report about Ceegee's hacking list, or Josh's project, which was so like Project Aardvark, till tomorrow night.

"Something's wrong, isn't it?" Mother sat down opposite me. I was conscious of how glad I was that it was she who was there, not Dad. I remembered how good it was to talk to her, and how much she already knew about Project Aardvark. "She's known about it from the beginning," Dad had said.

All at once I was telling my mother, in abbreviated form, of exactly what had gone on that afternoon.

When I was finished, Mother straightened and set her chin. "All right, let's say it straight out. You're afraid Ceegee's been hacking the alpha wave research, either taking it out of or putting it into SACAM. And you're afraid Josh is working with the master-mind behind the theft."

"Mother, I didn't say that —"

"You didn't have to. And you, yourself, have tapped into a lot of files you should not have entered, via numbers you aren't supposed to have."

I hadn't told her that part, but I should have remembered Mother could read me like a book. I felt the hot blood rush into my face. I said in a muffled voice, "You don't understand."

"Oh, yes, I do." Mother said deliberately. "Because your father's alpha research is so important, finding out the truth about who's been ripping it off or altering it is important. Because it is your father's work, it's important to you to help him — any way you can. But you hadn't bargained on that meaning spying on your friends, and that's tearing you apart. And some time soon, realizing what he's got you into is going to tear your father apart. He'll try to hide that behind professional detachment, but it won't work."

I knew exactly what she meant. "I feel as if I've gotten both of us caught in a trap," I said miserably.

"No, Sidney, you haven't," Mother said gently. "You've gotten caught in a difficult ethical dilemma, but that's another thing. Whoever ultimately is in the trap will be there because of the ethical choices that he made."

"I just don't want to be the one who sets or springs it." But I knew as I said it that it was already too late for that. I knew too much.

When the silence got too heavy, Mother broke it. "You've found some evidence that points to Ceegee." Even at that moment, I noticed she wasn't mentioning Josh. His name hung in the air between us. "You've jumped to the conclusion he's . . . implicated in some way, haven't you? Whatever happened to innocent until proven guilty?"

"Mom, that isn't fair."

"Isn't it? What would happen if you bury the evidence? You'll still have your suspicions. How do you think Ceegee would feel if he knew you believed the worst? Just as awful as you do suspecting him?" She waited. "You have the numbers, too, after all. *You* went hacking illegally into classified data banks."

"I got out of their computers immediately. I didn't change a thing. I didn't even read a thing, once I knew I wasn't into SACAM." I realized as I said that what I was implying. If I had gotten into SACAM, would I have kept reading till I did or did not find alpha wave material? The thought was disturbing.

To my relief, Mother did not get into that. "Could you prove that's all you did? Maybe it's all Ceegee's done, too." A small involuntary smile curved her lips. "I admit the thought of Ceegee not taking a look around does stretch the imagination. All I'm saying is everyone is entitled to the benefit of the doubt, and an open-minded search for evidence that will prove the truth one way or the other. And an opportunity to explain." She stopped. "Except there's no way to ask for an explanation, is there? Not without jeopardizing the secrecy of Project Aardvark."

Now you understand what I'm up against, I thought silently. I didn't say it. I said instead, in as bright a voice as I could manage, "Isn't dinner ready yet? I'm starved." I put something cheerful on the stereo.

I was saved from the fib about an appetite by Cordelia on the telephone. She sounded breathless. "Sidney? I'm running late, so can you be ready when we toot the horn?"

"Ready for what?"

"The basketball game," Cordelia said patiently. "Tonight's the last play-off before the tournament, and you promised me at lunch you'd go with me."

I had no recollection of that at all. "I'm not going," I said baldly.

Cordelia's voice quickened. "Sidney, is something wrong?"

"I'm just tired. And I don't want to give anybody ideas — you know."

"You'll give Ceegee the idea you don't even care about him fraternally if you're not on hand. This game really is a big thing. Steve would kill me if I didn't show, and I want to sit with you, so get ready."

"I can't. Really. Look, I have to go — we're in the middle of eating dinner." I hung up.

"You should go," Mother said. "It might clear the cobwebs."

"Mom, don't you start!"

Five minutes later the door opened and Cordelia walked in without even knocking.

Ice spangled her outer clothes, and her eyes were very bright. "Get your coat," she ordered. "If you don't come willingly, Mike's in the car and he's prepared to kidnap you by force. You're digging yourself a hole and burying yourself in it, and I'm not going to let that happen!"

Anything was better than sitting here with my whirling thoughts. I grabbed my coat and scarf and followed Cordelia out.

The noise in the gym reverberated around me. We were the visiting team and we were winning. I knew that even without watching, because Cordelia hugged me every time we made a basket. Parents and old grads were losing their cool. I could imagine what it was going to be like at the state tournament game on Friday. Even now, everybody was yelling and roaring and a couple of fights had broken out. It was a typical last game of the season, except that I was not a part of it. Fortunately, Cordelia didn't seem to notice.

The game went into overtime. Ceegee scored the winning points. The crowd went wild. Then everybody was pushing out of the bleachers, down toward the court. I spotted Heller Hazzard being hoisted to the shoulders of the team. I spotted Monahan. Cordelia grabbed my hand. "Come on! We're supposed to meet the guys in the parking lot. Steve and Ceegee had a bargain that if one of them made the winning points, the other one would buy the pizza!"

There was no getting away.

We drove back to Lakeland in the bosom of the team, and my silence continued to pass unnoticed. There were friends and family members around everywhere. Not Josh. Josh never came to athletic events. I sat in a little isolation booth of silence while tables were pushed together for a triumphal banquet. Twice, I caught Cordelia looking at me strangely. Once, I caught Ceegee, and it was I who dropped my eyes.

Then I was being driven home; I was letting Ceegee walk me to the door. I unlocked the door and submitted passively to Ceegee's risking a kiss good-night.

I closed the door after him and leaned against it in the dark as a desperate uneasiness, which had been crouching in the shadows, reached out to possess me. The game hadn't distracted me at all. The ethical question — the mystery, and my role in it — still waited to be faced.

Chapter 12

School the next day was like a carnival, because we were the contenders for the state basketball tournament. School pennants, banners, and posters blossomed everywhere. The team was being treated like superstars, and even Monahan was losing his cool. I walked through this general hysteria like the ghost at a wedding feast.

Amid the general euphoria, this mostly went unnoticed. Not by Cordelia, of course. She arrived that morning while Mother and I were still eating breakfast, and bore me off on a wave of cold air and determination. "We have to talk."

"About what?"

"About whatever it is that you're not telling me." Cordelia searched my face. "Something's wrong — it's getting wronger by the day — and last night you were ready to fall apart. Have you had a fight with Josh, is that it?"

"No! I'm just tired. And Ceegee —"

Cordelia brushed that away. "Cut the con. This is me, remember? I just want to know if there's anything I can do."

"There isn't. That is —" I stopped and thought. "Cordelia, you know how there's all this bragging about hacking. Have you ever heard anything that sounds like — like somebody's really doing it seriously?"

"I've heard till I'd like to scream at them to shut up, and if you ask me, it's mostly bragging. Kind of a macho thing. I'd discount half, and doubt half of the remainder." Cordelia looked at me closely. "You haven't found out there's any big-league theft-by-computer going on around here, have you?"

"How on earth would I find out about that? I just wondered."

"Now *I'm* worried," Cordelia said soberly.

At lunchtime Josh wanted to know how I was doing on the crackpot's programming. I stalled him. He reminded me about deadlines, and I reminded him he'd been the one who'd accepted the deadlines before knowing what the work entailed. We were still snapping at each other when Monahan's class began. Monahan interrupted this by hauling me off to his office.

"The administration knows about somebody using the school's computer time shares. I couldn't keep it hushed up anymore. There's been an audit, and someone's regularly been logging a few hours every day or so for the past month. Where's your father? I've been trying to telephone him, and that secretary of his keeps saying that he's not available."

"He's out of town. He's getting back to-night."

Monahan grunted. "And Jorgensen still off on his 'family business.'" That meant the trip to California. "This top secrecy of theirs may blow up any minute. I can't keep the police out of it much longer. I only got the administration to agree to hold off for a couple of days, while I did some investigating on my own. The school board would rather avoid a scandal if it could."

I was starting to feel very cold. I went back to Samantha, and Josh wanted to know what that was all about. I told him it wasn't his business, really, which did not go over well. "I hope you get *your* business wrapped up soon, since, as you've informed me, it takes priority over mine," he said stiffly. "You can have the Gemini all afternoon. I have business elsewhere." That meant his course at the university.

Between classes I called home and Dad's office. Mother was out. Dad's secretary had heard from him; he was going to be away an extra day. "He's gotten a lead on some information for his research work," she said.

That could mean anything. After school I did not go to the computer lab. I went straight home, and put a telephone call through to the hotel where Dad was staying. They didn't know where he was. I put down the phone and thought hard.

Dad was at a medical convention. I located

the brochures, and they stated clearly that the convention did not get out until 5 p.m. That was only an hour and a half away — I looked again, and my breath quickened. No. The convention was in the Midwest, in a different time zone. I had an extra hour. And there was something in the brochure about a computer center at the university hospital where the convention was based. Where computers would be, I'd bet anything there would be my father.

I rummaged in the files in Dad's study and, sure enough, there was a data bank telephone number by which the hospital could be accessed by computer modem. I took the six steps up to my office in three bounds, made the connection, and started keyboarding.

DR. S. S. WEBSTER. MODEM CONNECTOR LIST FOUND & CHECKED. DATA BANK WE'RE INTERESTED IN NOT AMONG THEM. GOLFING BUDDY SAYS HACKING BEING LOOKED INTO. NOT OFFICIAL YET. ADVISE YOUR DATA PROCESSOR.

I felt like an idiot trying to be cryptic, but at this point I was seeing spies in corners.

Within fifteen minutes an answer started appearing on our home monitor. Dad *was* at the computer center, and he wasn't wasting time with a telephone.

CHECK MY OFFICE & WHERE YOU TOOK TESTS. HAVE MY FILES ACCESSED. TAKE MY NUMBER & MAKE PRINTOUTS. HOME TOMORROW.

If Dad wanted me to access his private files, things were even more serious than I had realized. All of a sudden, being alone in my own house felt scary. I left a note for Mother on the refrigerator and started towards the hospital, taking the attaché case to lock the printouts in. Before I left the house I stuck all the Project Aardvark material from the attaché case underneath my mattress.

I didn't have any difficulty at the hospital; I told Dad's secretary I was supposed to meet my mother there and could I wait in Dad's office. Since I'd done this before, she let me. I took out the address book I'd brought from home, which contained Dad's private numbers, and I accessed the hospital mainframe via his personal computer. I felt like a burglar, and I very carefully did not get into anything but what Dad had told me to. The Aardvark file in the hospital mainframe had been accessed twice in the past week. Whoever had done it had identified himself (herself?) as Dad.

I got a printout of the material in the file and changed the entry code. That should stall the hacker for a day or so. Then, feeling very cold, I told the secretary that I'd called home and wasn't going to wait there for Mother, after all. How many lies I'd told this time, I had no idea.

It was an indication of my state of mind that this time I was wondering if I was being followed. I spooked at footsteps in the hospital corridor, but when I looked around it was only two comfortable middle-aged ladies on their way out after visiting a patient. I went to the university and found the lab in the psychology department where I'd taken those tests of my alleged ESP. Nobody was around who recognized me. Fortunately I had my school ID card, which had my photo, and nobody in the psych office knew my father. But nobody could or would tell me whether there was any information being held there for him.

"Where's the university library?" I asked suddenly, and the building was pointed out for me through the window. Snow was beginning to fall as I trudged over.

Where there were libraries, nowadays, there often were computers. In college libraries, so I'd heard, there frequently were computers for student use that could be activated by putting quarters in a slot. Just the way libraries made electronic typewriters available for students. So it was there, in a little room off the bookstacks with college students hammering out term papers on either side of me, that I connected up a modem when the librarians weren't looking and got a printout from Dad's university files. They, too, had been entered during the past week.

I didn't look at the printouts to see what, if anything, the hacker(s) got. I just locked them up in the attaché case, and made very sure any memory the battered computer had was cleared, and plunged outside again. My one thought was to get home, and have my mother be there, and hope that Dad would phone.

The simplest way home from the university was around the lake. It was twilight now, but the streetlights made pools of yellow glow, and a couple of kids were trying to play hockey on the snowy lake. I could hear their voices and their laughter. I walked rapidly, stumbling over frozen snow lumps. I came to the point where the road and sidewalk curved to the left, around a stretch of park, and a path led off through the snowy parkland, following the lakeshore to the right. It was lonelier, but it was a much shorter way to home. And the snow gave back a luminous glow, and there were streetlights, and the kids were on the lake, and I wanted very much to get back home.

I started across the park.

I hadn't gone ten feet when I had it again — that sensation that I was being followed. I could feel the hackles on my neck rise, and my feet felt like blocks of ice. Doggedly, I kept moving them. This area was wide open; I was visible. I could get out of the park faster by continuing on than if I had turned back and had to walk the long way round. So I kept going.

I kept going, and I heard nothing, but my uneasiness increased. Maybe that was just because my heart was pounding. Deliberately, I quieted my heart and pulse, the way I had to do if I wanted to induce an alpha state. It helped. So did reminding myself that I had no reason to expect trouble. But I kept remembering too many things my father had said.

And then a voice said, "You're going home kind of late, aren't you?"

A figure emerged out of the dimness. It wasn't one of the hackers. It was the school custodian, the new one who'd been annoyed about my working in the computer lab and about the snake.

I said, "Yes," shortly, and kept on going. To my dismay, he fell in beside me.

"You weren't working after school today."

"That's right," I said. I didn't want to be rude and start anything. I didn't want to encourage further conversation, so I just kept moving. To my dismay, he did also. He wasn't fresh; he wasn't threatening. He was just *there*.

He smiled, and then I did feel scared. It wasn't a frightening smile, it was another kind entirely. "I've kind of missed you, not being there after school lately. Though what a cute little girl like you wants to waste time around computers for beats me. Haven't you got better things to do?"

All at once, he was definitely too close. Not doing anything, just looming. The path was narrower; I could not get past him. And then I heard footsteps pounding through the snow, and a familiar voice.

"Sorry I'm late! I hope you didn't think you'd been stood up!"

It was Josh, barrelling over from the direction of the university. He didn't sound like Josh. He sounded like Steve would when he had a date with Cordelia and had kept her waiting. He braked to a stop on the other side of me, tucked his arm through mine, and said, "Come on, I'm starved."

We nodded to the custodian and marched off.

I was shaking, I couldn't help it, and Josh felt it clear through our winter coats. He marched me in the direction of that built-in seat, brushed the snow off for us, and demanded, "What was that all about?"

"I don't know. I guess he was — coming on to me."

"He could get fired for that, if you report it. Are you going to?"

"I don't know." I looked at him and said through chattering teeth, "What are you doing here?"

"Coming home from class at the U. I saw you, and then I saw that creep, and I figured something fishy was going on. What are *you* doing here?"

"Coming home from the U. also."

"I thought you were going to be hammering out your work-for-hire all afternoon." Josh stopped. "Or was that about your work-for-hire? You doing research or hacking the university's data files?"

"I would have thought that was more your

department." I don't know what made me say that; it just came out. Josh's eyes narrowed. "Exactly what is that supposed to mean?"

I chose my words with care. "If I hit home, you know what it means. If I didn't, then it doesn't matter. Why did you ask me if I went hacking into data banks?"

"Isn't that what half the computer freaks we know spend their time either trying or bragging about? I've been kind of worried sometimes about the security of those data banks."

"Like SACAM?"

Josh grew very still. "What do you know about SACAM?"

"I know what it is, and apparently you do, too."

"I've done work for firms who use it." Josh peered off through the snow towards the frozen lake. "Something very fishy's going on," he said at last. "You're not acting like yourself. And too many weird things are going on. That snake in your book bag. That guy just now. He's not a dirty old man. No insult intended, but you're too young to interest him, especially with his job involved. And SACAM. Does that work you're doing involve SACAM?"

"You know I can't tell you that."

"Just tell me this," Josh said, very seriously, "is the work anything that would be vulnerable to rip-off? Is there any reason anyone could want to scare you off of it, or off the computer lab?"

I didn't answer. Apparently I didn't have to. Josh's face tightened, and he stood up. "Come on."

"Where?"

"I'm walking you home. When we get there we can get some work done, if you want to. No," he corrected himself, "first we're going to the Pizza Palace. We're going to show ourselves there acting normal, as if nothing's scared you and there's nothing important on our minds. Then, if anybody is — keeping an eye on you — there'll be nothing suspicious."

So he thought maybe I'd been followed, too!

The Pizza Palace was steamy and noisy — the basketball team and hangers-on had arrived, and a stereo blared. I phoned Mother to tell her where I was and with whom, and when I got back to our booth Josh had ordered lavishly.

"You could have asked if I liked anchovies," I said when a pizza with everything arrived.

"You didn't tell me."

"It wouldn't have occurred to you to ask, I suppose. You just take over." If Josh thought we should show ourselves acting normal, we sure were doing it — arguing. Only we weren't just putting on a show about the pizza. I knew it, and Josh knew it. We were talking about what had happened at the lake.

"It seems to me there are a lot of things

you haven't told me," Josh said quietly.

"It works both ways." A thought flickered into my mind. If that custodian could have been in the park either by chance or not, what about Josh?

I started to shiver again, and Josh's eyes changed. There was concern in them I'd scarcely seen before. And something else, too. Alarm. He put his hand over mine.

"Sidney —"

I tried to pull my hand away, and his tightened on it. "Don't pull off, and I don't mean just literally. You can't escape facts by going into another state of consciousness."

"What did you say?"

We stared at each other, motionless, breathing hard. Then a grip like a vice clamped Josh's shoulder.

"Get your hands off the lady, creep," Ceegee ordered.

"It's okay," I said in a low voice.

"No, it's not. This guy's been annoying you ever since he hit town, and it's time he cooled it. He's making a public spectacle!" Talk about scenes, Ceegee was clearly spoiling for one. His voice was too loud. I flashed a plea for help in the direction of Steve and Cordelia, and managed to get my own hand free. I also kicked Josh underneath the table.

"Look, Ceegee, this is a personal matter," I said in as normal a tone as I could muster. "It doesn't have anything to do with you."

"It does have to do with me. Anything

that affects me does, and I'm fed up with not being able to do anything about it. So I'm warning —"

It was like a nightmare. Other than the blare of the stereo, the place was ominously silent. Everybody's ears were straining to hear the "fun."

"Keep your warnings to yourself," Josh said, very quietly. "The lady doesn't need them. And anything you have to say to me could be better settled elsewhere."

"You wouldn't have the guts!"

I knew, too well, that reckless note in Ceegee's voice. Blessedly, Steve and Cordelia were there. Cordelia said, with just the right note of amusement, "Come on, you guys! You promised to get me home before my dad gets sore."

"Sure," Steve said. His eyes flicked over Josh, then he turned to Ceegee. "This guy's not worth the effort. Come on, Ceegee, let's get the girls home."

Josh rose.

"Don't," I said in a low voice. He ignored it.

"I said I'd see you got home safely. I'm quite capable of making sure you're safe — including from animals whose brains are in their fists."

The jocks breathed fire.

I had again this disembodied sense of watching. Josh striding towards the door like a macho prince, as if taking for granted that I would follow. Myself jumping up, crying out, trying to catch Ceegee's arm. Ceegee shaking me off. The jocks marching towards the door in phalanx, with Cordelia and me darting after like the tail of a kite. A considerable audience fell in behind us.

The night air was cold. Behind us, the stereo blared distantly, and the neon sign winked, red and blue. I could not reach out. I could not speak. Ceegee squared off, his long arms waving wildly. I remember wondering whether he'd stopped off for a beer after practice, or whether he was punch-drunk on basketball success. Or on anger. Josh stood very still, incongruous in his VIP business clothes and that crazy coat.

Ceegee's right arm swung out. And stopped, caught, pinioned in a vicelike grip. Josh's move had been so smooth and sudden it had not been seen.

"Sidney's not a piece of property. You don't own her, so stop embarrassing her by treating her like you do," Josh said distinctly.

For an instant, both were motionless. Then Ceegee tried to move. And was flipped, smoothly, effortlessly, head over heels. He landed sprawling and breathless in a pile of snow. The air was electric, and in the stillness Josh brushed himself off and turned to me. "Shall I see you home?"

"I have some unfinished business here," I said grimly.

"As you like." Josh tightened, bowed faintly, and was off into the night.

Ceegee was being pulled out of the snowbank, rubbing his shoulder, and covering his defeat with wisecracks. "Who'd have thought it?" he muttered, looking after Josh.

"Not you," I said icily. "Not any of you. Just because he's not the kind of athlete that you're used to. . . Josh is right, your brains are in your fists." My eyes traveled back to Ceegee, and I framed my words very carefully. "You don't own me. You can't barge in and protect me unless I want it. I'm sorry, but that's just the way it is."

Even as I said it, I was aware of several things. I *didn't* want it, not from Ceegee. And it was more than half my fault he believed — or wanted to believe — I did. And where Josh was concerned —

I turned away, clutching my belongings, including the attaché, and started after Josh. But by the time I reached the corner, he was lost from sight.

Chapter 13

We didn't do any work together that night.

I went home and worked on Project Aardvark data on the computer, and made so many mistakes that I finally gave up and spent the evening watching TV. I couldn't concentrate on anything. I felt uneasy. Not just because of what had happened in the park, but what had happened at the Pizza Palace.

The incident in the park was more clearcut — or was it? I snapped off the TV and threw myself on my back across the bed, considering. A man who knew me from his work at school had tried to get too chummy. I hadn't handled it well. It had gotten sticky, and Josh had come and rescued me. Those were the facts.

But there were feelings and suspicions, as well as facts. Grown men who worked for the school didn't usually make passes at the schoolgirls, and that had been a pass. *Or a threat.* The word leaped out of my unconscious, startling me. Threat? Maybe. Maybe an attempt to scare me away from hanging around the computer room again. Because I had been scared. I didn't like one bit the idea of encountering Wiggins there again.

I'd been scared even before Wiggins spoke to me, hadn't I? Scared walking along the lakeshore, which I'd wandered in absolute safety, in light and darkness, for many years. I hadn't felt safe today. Had I been picking up vibes, or was working on Project Aardvark starting to get to me?

And then there was that little fracas at the Pizza Palace. It wouldn't have happened if I'd handled the situation better. Josh had been feeling good, feeling like a knight rescuing a maiden in distress, and the maiden had treated his kindness like an insult.

And Ceegee . . . Josh had made him look like a fool in front of me, and he deserved better. Sure, Ceegee had underestimated Josh. But as for his proprietary attitude towards me, I had only myself to blame. The way I'd led him on . . . The memory flooded back, making me feel hot. Computer thief or not, Ceegee was an old friend. He'd come to my rescue as Josh had, because he thought I needed it and because he cared.

There were a lot of people it was not going to be easy for me to face.

I didn't have to avoid Ceegee the next day, because he was avoiding me. So were the other jocks. Nothing ostentatious; no outright snubs. They just weren't around, or else weren't looking in my direction. I ought to have been relieved; instead I was both dismayed and angry.

Cordelia acted exactly as she always did, but when she spotted me by my locker on my way to lunch she inquired beneath her breath, "How *are* you?"

"Holding pattern. I think."

"Mmm," Cordelia said comprehensively. "Well, hang in there." She looked at me, then away. "You were right, you know. What you said to Ceegee, and — everything."

"I could have found a better way to say it. I could have — not created the situation."

"No use crying over spilt milk. Anyway, if I know you, you had your reasons." When I didn't answer, Cordelia added, "It was bound to happen sooner or later. And it's probably a good thing it did. The guys got a big jolt, I can tell you."

Cordelia linked her arm through mine. "Come on, let's go eat."

Coward that I was, I chickened out of Monahan's computer class by getting an emergency pass to the library to do research for an English class assignment.

I couldn't chicken out of working after school because the need to keep up-to-date on Project Aardvark was becoming urgent, and I'd been spending too much time lately on my work with Josh.

I had the lab to myself, and I was just getting into a good alpha wave conversation with Samantha when the door slamming at the other end of the room broke the trance. Wiggins? For an instant I felt clammy. Then I forced a look, and felt clammy for another reason. Josh was coming towards me briskly.

"I got the chemical stuff out by express mail just now," he said matter-of-factly. "Let's lay out the next batch of work for that other outfit." He was acting as if nothing out of the ordinary had happened yesterday, and I felt the tension oozing out of me.

"Yes. Sure. I'll just clear what I was doing."

"We could have used your system disk," Josh commented as I locked my disks away.

"It only takes a few minutes to change them. It's better to keep our businesses totally separate." I vacated the chair before Samantha so he could boot her up, but instead he pulled another chair up to an empty table.

"This stuff's weird. I think you'd better look it over first." Josh took out a pile of printouts and spread them out. I joined him, looked, and got an uneasy feeling in my stomach.

"What *is* this, anyway?"

"Some sort of medical-pharmaceutical research. Pretty far out; not pure science. Mostly physics." Josh's tone had a faint tinge of contempt. I gave him a look.

"I know it's physics; I get straight A's. But some of this is stuff I don't recognize." That was a lie. I recognized some of the material as having a direct relationship to what

I'd tried to process at home last night for Project Aardvark.

"Nobody would recognize it. I think there's a gnome in a lab somewhere in Silicon Valley who dreams this all up. What we're supposed to do is chart a correlation between the experiments they claim they've made."

He sounded so absolutely disinterested that I began to believe he really didn't know what the research was all about. Maybe his employer hadn't told him. The possibility reassured me, and the notion of him as an innocent pawn amused me.

"I think I see what they want," I said, relenting. It wasn't going to be easy to process the same data in a different way from what I'd done for Dad. I toyed with the idea of a spot of sabotage, but stopped in time. Maybe this *was* independent research — another scientist also working in secrecy on the same premise at the same time. I thought for a moment.

"How about a bar graph? Like this." I seated myself at Samantha and started working. Samantha liked doing graphics and cooperated beautifully.

Josh watched over my shoulder. "That's fine," he said. "You do the graphs and the final write-up. I hate having to fool with graphics. I'll work on the mathematical equations."

"Yes, numbers are more dependable, aren't they?" I murmured dryly. Josh grinned.

"Okay, so I like things I can count on to behave predictably. Nothing wrong with that, is there?"

"Not a thing. So long as you're human enough to throw a curve now and then to keep people guessing. That was karate yesterday, wasn't it?"

"Tai Kwan Doh. There's a slight difference."

"What else do you do that's — slightly different?"

Josh shrugged. "Archery. Fencing. Darts. Not team sports."

"I noticed. What else?"

"Play the piano. Mostly jazz; I like the mathematical progressions. Go to concerts sometimes. Rig computers to do crazy things." He grinned.

"You're kidding."

"Get the first five bar graphs done and I'll teach — what do you call her, Samantha? — to set off the fire alarm during class tomorrow."

"You wouldn't!"

"Watch me!"

I didn't know what had gotten into either of us. Relief, probably, that the subject of Ceegee's nosedive had been broached and passed. I'd learned more about Joshua J. Rivington III in the past five minutes than I had in the past several weeks. Correction, learned more in the past twenty-four hours. I wondered, with equivocal feelings, what he'd found out about me.

We worked in silence for an hour, I on Samantha, he on a nearby IBM. "Done," I said at last. "You?"

"Take a look at some of these, will you?"

"Load them into Samantha. I have your disks in them anyway, and if your new data's added to them, I'll be able to start graphing it first thing next time."

Josh did so, then he retrieved the new equations onto the monitor, and we studied them together. I squinted, then shook my head.

"What's the matter? Did I do something wrong?" Josh demanded.

"I don't think so. There's just something that struck me —" I shook my head again. "I've lost it. You promised me you'd teach Samantha to set the fire alarm."

I never thought that he would, let alone could, do so. Yet there he was, suit jacket off and sleeves rolled up, removing the wall plates from buzzer, fire alarm, ceiling light, using a pair of scissors as a screwdriver.

"Don't you need to string wires, or something?" I asked.

Josh shook his head. "The Gemini has an electromagnetic field of fifty feet. Now if we just do this —" He was very busy inside the wall cavities, then went back to Samantha. "And code in a key word for each function. Say kappa for buzzer, sigma for overhead light, delta for alarm."

"Say *finish* to our using the lab, if somebody finds those wall plates off."

Josh's eyes glinted. "You ready to try out the fire alarm?"

"*NO!* We don't want the whole adminis-stration on our necks!"

"I'll just set the clock then," Josh relented. He flexed his fingers, started hitting keys. The hands on the classroom clock began turning. I gazed, open-mouthed. Then I jumped.

"Stop that or you'll set the buzzer for class periods going!" The look on his face told me he knew that fact very well. I grabbed his arms. "I mean that — cut it out! You want to bring Monahan in here, or Hazzard? Hazzard's always hanging around here some-where."

Josh pried my fingers from his arms and rubbed the bruises. "Lady, you pack a mean grip, don't you? Why is Hazzard always around?"

"Because he doesn't like going home. If you're black and blue, it serves you right. My wrist is, too, so we're even. Look, can I take some of this material we've just been working on home to study?"

"I'll make you a printout."

"I'll make the printout. You put those wall switches back the way they were."

"If I fool around with them again now, Monahan could catch us. Basketball practice should be getting out any minute. I hadn't planned to stay this late." *Meaning he didn't care to run into the jocks again,* I thought, amused. "Anyway," Josh added, triumphantly," nobody could set those gadgets off via Samantha unless they knew the code words and had my program disk."

Our disks, I corrected silently. While Josh was rolling down his sleeves I was surreptitiously making backup disk copies for myself.

"At least set the clock straight," I suggested demurely, and Josh did so, first disconnecting the electric plug so the buzzer could not be set off. He screwed all the switch plates back in place. "They'll be okay so long as nobody keys Greek letters into Samantha," he said smugly, grinning. "Are you ready to go?"

A faint chill swept me. "I'll close up here. You go ahead."

Josh's smile faded. "Are you sure? I don't want you walking home alone. Not after yesterday."

"I'll be all right, really. I can call Mom for a ride." There was something I had to do, for him as much as for me, and I could not do it with him there. He hesitated, but at last he went.

I locked the door's dead bolt after him, so I would be safe. Monahan and the jocks were in the gym. Not to mention Heller Hazzard, who was bound to be around someplace. Mr. Jorgensen was probably in his office — no, he wasn't back yet from California. No one would have any way of knowing if I got in trouble here.

They'd know if the alarms and buzzers

went off. Feeling self-conscious, I set Samantha up to obey the Greek letter codes if needed.

What I had stayed for was to check the copies I'd made of Josh's system and data disks, in the hope of clearing Josh from association with Project Aardvark data. I also wanted to have another look at that page of formulas which had stirred something in my mind. First I had to find it, which presented problems. Josh programmed in a regular computer language, but he had his own original filing code, known to him alone. I studied the index and menu listings on his data disk, and it occurred to me he was being just too cute. Maybe secrecy was necessary to protect against industrial theft, but wasn't he carrying things too far?

There *was* one way to find anything hidden on a disk, without knowing file names, and that was to scan the entire disk, as repairmen and quality control inspectors did. And I just happened to know how to do it, thanks to Ceegee's coaching.

I started flashing through the keys.

Samantha's monitor blinked and sputtered; it began flashing forth an insane array of letters, numbers, symbols. I let the screen fill, then punched STOP and started scanning. Page by page I went through, skimming rapidly, knowing all the gibberish would show up on a printout but wanting to check it, right now, all the same.

I found physics formulas, the correlations

Josh had been working on; nothing else. My graphs should be coming up soon, I thought absently, punching up the next page.

My fingers froze on the keys.

The gibberish on the screen had become familiar, so familiar that I was suddenly fumbling through my attaché case, searching for the printout of the gobbledygook I had first found in Samantha's memory.

What was on the screen now was not a replica. Some of the formulas were the same. And the word *aardvark*. But there were other formulas that made the hair rise on my neck, made me paw through the attaché case again, then sit back, feeling weak and cold.

The data on the screen had not come out of Samantha's own memory. I had checked *that* before I started working this afternoon, some time before Josh came in. I had cleared Samantha's memory completely before letting Josh boot up.

And the data had not been part of my own work, now or earlier. It had triggered my memory for one reason and one reason only. The fomulas were part of the newest work on Project Aardvark, given to me that morning by my father, in a printout Thor Jorgensen had made on his office computer just last night.

Chapter 14

Like an automaton, I methodically made printouts, made backup disks, locked everything into the supposed security of the attaché case, and went out into the night.

Where was I going? I didn't know.

Not home. Mom was meeting Dad at the airport downtown after her hospital auxiliary meeting got out. At home I would be alone with my own thoughts. At home Josh might be calling on his telephone.

My feet started moving. The wind stung my face. I bent against it, doggedly putting one boot before the other, hugging myself against the chill. Presently I found myself before Cordelia's house, and I went up the slippery path and rang the bell.

"Hey, this is great!" Cordelia said as she opened the door. Then her smile vanished. "Sidney, what's wrong?"

"Nothing's wrong. I'd just like to come in and get warm for a little while, if you don't mind."

"Of course we mind. We'll even charge you for your dinner if you'll stay. Come inside and get those boots off, you idiot." Cordelia peeled me out of my wet things and steered me to a kitchen chair. "You're in luck. Mom's made stew, and there's plenty. We'll be eating in half an hour. Dad's not home yet, neither is Mike, and Mom's upstairs beating the little kids into doing homework."

"Steve's not coming over, is he?"

"Uh-uh. I decided that little run-in you and Josh staged at the Pizza Palace gave me the opening to drive a few truths home, too. I don't like guys acting as if they own me, any more than you do." Cordelia gave the stew pot a stir and asked casually, "That's not still eating you, is it?"

"No. Anyway, I don't believe you and Steve are on the outs. You can trust Steve, and you know it."

"Sure, I can trust him. To be who he is, and what he is." Cordelia's tone was teasing, but her eyes sobered. "That's all any of us can really trust in anyone, isn't it? To be themselves?"

"That's okay if you know who they are."

"If I don't after five years of going around with the guy, I'm in big trouble."

"What would you do if you didn't? Cordelia, stop looking at me like that and answer me. I'm serious."

"Yes, I can see you are." Cordelia sat down. "I guess I'd give him the benefit of the doubt. And if I still wasn't sure, and needed

157

to be, I'd ask him face to face."

"You sound like my mother. Innocent till proven guilty."

"Well, that's what we want for ourselves, isn't it? Anyway," Cordelia went on more lightly, "you've known Ceegee even longer than I've known Steve, so you should be able to trust your judgment. Or isn't it Ceegee we're talking about?"

"I don't know. Cordelia, thanks anyway, but I don't think I'll stay for dinner." I struggled back into my boots, conscious of Cordelia watching me with troubled eyes.

Our house was dark when I reached it. I let myself in, locked the door behind me, and then, feeling self-conscious, made the rounds of the other doors and double-bolted them as well. I closed the curtains before turning on all the lights. A note on the kitchen table indicated the refrigerator contained a casserole awaiting microwaving for my dinner. I ignored it and went upstairs, and all the things whirling around in my head went with me. I was afraid of those things. I was afraid of being here alone. I was afraid of going out alone, but after fifteen minutes that was what I did.

I walked the six blocks to the high school, where basketball practice was in session, and I kept on walking. Downtown, past the Pizza Palace, along the several blocks to where the garden apartments stood nearby the railroad. I didn't know which one I was looking for, but my steps were not purposeless. I went from one doorway to another, reading the names on the mailboxes until I found the one I wanted and rang the bell.

I heard footsteps clattering on stairs inside, and the door opened. Josh stood there, surprise changing into pleasure. "Webster! Come on in, I was just trying to call you."

"What about?"

"That can wait. Tell me what brought you here, first." Josh suddenly looked sheepish and stepped back. "Sorry, I'm not much good at playing host. Come on upstairs first."

He led the way, and I followed. He took my coat. He left me in the small, pleasant living room while he hung it up. He came back, and gestured to a chair. "What is it? Nothing went wrong with the material you took home to work on, did it?"

I didn't answer, and I didn't sit, and something changed in his face. "You didn't come here to quit on me again, did you?" He made it sound like a joke, but it wasn't.

"I came here to ask you about this." I unlocked my attaché case and took out a printout, which I handed him in silence.

Josh looked at it and frowned, and all at once his eyes were wary. "Where did you get this?"

"Off the data disk you *didn't* give me. I made a backup copy . . . in case I needed any information that was on it to clarify the material I was working on."

Josh's eyebrow went up, and his voice was icy cold. He was very angry. "I don't appreciate having people poking through my private work."

"It's not your private work. You brought me into it — as an equal. And don't tell me this isn't part of that mental telepathy communication research, because I recognize parts of it. That wasn't all I recognized." I dipped into the attaché case again. "Have you ever seen this?"

Josh, still furious, took a brief glance, then looked closer. "Where did you get *this*?" He wasn't angry anymore. He was like a scientist scenting a clue.

"I got it out of Samantha's own memory, days ago. It has some of the same formulas we were working with today. That must have been what caught my attention this afternoon." I said abruptly, "Josh, what does *aardvark* mean?"

"How the devil should I know? Some kind of animal, isn't it?"

"The word showed up in that printout from your data disk," I said steadily.

"I know; I can see. I haven't even looked at that stuff yet," Josh said impatiently. "It just came to me this morning through the modem. Why does it matter to you so much, anyway?"

I didn't answer. We stood glaring at each other for a minute, then Josh broke off and ran his fingers through his hair. "This is crazy. It's totally crazy. Here we are at each other's throats again, and for no reason. Over an aardvark, for heaven's sake! How are we going to do things together if one of us is always on the defensive?"

"Maybe we aren't going to."

"Oh, yes, we are." Josh's smile began slowly, spread across his face and up to his eyes, as my heart turned over. "Stay here. I have something to show you." He bolted out.

"Read this," he said, returning to thrust a letter in my hands.

I read it. I looked up at him, and when I spoke my voice sounded odd. "The pharmaceutical company's offering you a job."

"You got it! No more hustling work," Josh said happily, "or all the other headaches of self-employment. Oh, I still intend to own my own company in a few years, but this is a start. It'll give me good credentials. See, they don't want me to start till summer, so if I knock myself out I can graduate here first. I can take college courses at night out there in California." He saw my face, and added quickly, "We'll still be working together on this ESP project now, you know. I'll probably have other work for you, too, until I move. After I start the job in California I can probably throw some free-lance work your way, if you want it. You might think about college in California, too."

He had it all planned out. He was so *sure*. I just looked at him, and then I was saying, carefully, deliberately, "Do you really think they'll hire you if they know you've been involved in computer theft of research?"

It didn't penetrate right away. In slow

motion I saw Josh's eyes go from blank to puzzled to outraged and disbelieving. "*What* did you say?"

"You heard me. The material on those printouts I just showed you came from a research project of my father's that he's been working on for several years." I was burning my bridges, and my father's also, but he wasn't here to be consulted. "*I* know what *aardvark* stands for, even if you don't." Something tightened inside me. "Or maybe you do. Maybe you know just what you're involved in, and don't even care."

A little muscle started pulsing next to Josh's eye. "If you think I'm involved in something illegal, or unethical —"

"I don't know *what* to think, do I, until you tell me?"

There was a wall of a few inches of thin air between us. We stood there staring through it, breathing hard, and at that moment we heard footsteps on the stairs.

"That's my mother," Josh said, not moving. "Shut up about this, will you? Just shut up."

"Josh? I wasn't sure whether you'd be home. Have you —" A slim dark woman stepped in, then stopped, her face softening with surprise and pleasure.

"Mother, this is Sidney Webster. She's doing some computer work for me," Josh said stiffly.

"We've met. I work at the library, but I didn't know you were Josh's Sidney." So that was why she looked familiar, I thought, as she held out her hand. "I'm glad to meet you. And I'm glad you're here. Josh seldom has friends visit." Mrs. Rivington hung up her coat and came back, smiling. "I can smell that Josh has been cooking dinner. Will you join us? Oh, of course, you've probably already eaten. When I work this shift, I get home from the library so late."

"I haven't eaten. I'd love to stay," I said clearly, and avoided Josh's eyes.

It was a strained, awkward meal, eaten by candlelight on a lace-covered drop-leaf table in the living room. Josh's goulash was delicious. We talked about books. Josh didn't care for fiction, and that was about the only thing I learned.

"Aren't you going to tell your mother about the job offer?" I asked at last, boldly.

Josh's eyes were furious but he said coldly, "Yes, of course," and got the letter. Mrs. Rivington read it and started looking alarmed. "Don't worry. I'm not dropping out of high school," John said flatly. "I can work and still do college."

"We have plenty of time to think about it later," Mrs. Rivington said just as firmly. I recognized the signs of an incipient family battle.

"I'd better be getting home," I said.

Josh promptly got my things, and his mother told me to come again, and that Josh would see me to the door. He didn't want to, but couldn't find any way out. In the little vestibule downstairs, we faced each other.

"Well?" I asked.

He was back to the Joshua J. Rivington III I had met on the first day of the semester in the computer store — distant and cold. "Well what?"

"Well, you know darn well what!" I saw the muscles in his face and neck grow taut. I knew — no, wait a minute; I didn't really *know* anything about him, did I? Not for sure. And I was suddenly angry. "Are you going to break down and tell me what this mental telepathy work we're doing is *really* all about? Or are you going to force me to believe you're actively involved in the computer theft?"

"If that's what you choose to believe," Josh said coldly.

"I'm not choosing anything! I'm trying to find out! I'm trying to help. I came over here to give you a chance to explain, but if you can't or won't trust me with the truth —"

"Why should I?" Josh burst out. "You've obviously made up your own mind already. *You* stole data from *my* data disk. Why should *I* trust *you*?"

"That's the whole point! We got into this — both of us — before we really knew each other." I was talking about the computer work, and a lot more also, and we both knew it. "Now we can't just run back to the way things were before it happened. We have to take each other on faith."

My voice changed. "Maybe that's not

what's really bothering you. Maybe it's that you've run into some things you can't analyze into neat, tidy, bloodless piles of data, with that logical mind of yours. Or maybe your drive for money, and your need to have absolute control, are in conflict. Because you need me to make money on this project, don't you? Whatever it really is, and whoever it's for. So I guess, Mr. Joshua J. Rivington III, you're going to have to consult Samantha one more time. Only there's one more variable you'll have to factor in."

Josh asked involuntarily, his voice cracking, "What's that?"

I had started out the door, but I swung around to face him in the ring of light. "By the time you make up your mind to tell me the truth, maybe I won't be able to believe it!"

Chapter 15

Snow was swirling in the air, so that the streetlights glowed through halos. The neon signs on storefronts winked. I hugged the attaché against me and kept moving. My brain seemed to hover somewhere outside my body, watching it struggle against the drifts. *I'm in alpha state now*, I thought vaguely. But there was no satisfaction. There was only a numbness and a creeping fear.

And then, suddenly, I was not so much alone. A car turned out from a side street, was cruising along very slowly in my direction. I increased my pace, and the car accelerated. I had reached a fairly deserted residential area now. What should I do? Run to one of the houses and ring a doorbell? Try to double back to town, where the Pizza Palace would offer the safety of people and a telephone?

The car's headlights suddenly switched to brights, and the beam impaled me. There was the sound of a door opening. My feet were like lead weights.

"*Sidney!*" It was Cordelia's voice. Within seconds Cordelia and her brother Mike were there, surrounding me with safety, hurrying me back to Mike's old car with anxiety and concern.

"Where have you been? Your parents have been worried sick. When they called me, and found how long you'd been gone from our place —" Cordelia broke off, searching my face. "Are you sick, or hurt, or what?"

"I'm fine. Please, just get me home."

"We're going to," Mike said grimly. "Your Dad's got half the neighborhood out looking for you — us and Ceegee and Steve and Lord knows who else." He skidded around a corner, went up the Prospect Street hill at far too great a speed, and screeched into our own driveway.

"She's here!" Cordelia called, as the side door flew open. Lights streamed from all windows, and Mother came running out through the snowdrifts, coatless and bootless. I hugged her hard.

"Mom, I'm okay, really. Where's Dad?"

"On the telephone, trying to force the police to start a search."

I broke free and ran towards the house. "I have to stop him before he tells them."

I burst into the kitchen, and everybody there froze like statues. Monahan, puffing a cigar and drinking coffee. Thor Jorgensen, making notes. Dad at the telephone, suddenly snapping, "She just walked in," and dropping the phone into the receiver. I cut him off before he could speak.

"Dad, I have to talk to you. Right now. Alone."

Blessedly, he responded as a surgeon would to an emergency signal. His eyes cased the room and lit on Cordelia and her brother standing in the doorway. "Mike, can we take your car?" Mike tossed the key, and Dad pulled on his sheepskin jacket and hurried me outside. I half fell into the front seat, watched my father struggling with the ignition, and started giggling helplessly.

"This is all so silly —"

"Not now. Wait till we get away from here," Dad said shortly. He got the engine going, backed out of the drive, and drove the mile and a half to the lakeshore before putting the car in park and turning in the seat.

"I wanted to be sure we weren't in any room or vehicle that could be bugged."

I stared at him. "You don't really think —"

"I'll have everything checked tomorrow, just in case. I don't know what I think, but I know what I was afraid of when your mother and I came home and couldn't find you. No dinner eaten, no note, no telephone call."

"I should have. I'm sorry. I had . . . things I had to think about, and then get straight.

Only I'm still not straight about them. I'm more confused." I stared out the window at the lake. It was an alien world now, remote and still. I drew my breath in painfully.

"You said we had to talk immediately." It was a gentle reminder, but it brought back the sense of urgency. I turned and looked at Dad with anguish.

"I feel like a — a traitor, and a spy. But I have to tell you. Dad, I found some more Project Aardvark materials this afternoon. A rehash of what was in Samantha earlier, and a direct copy of the material you just gave me."

"In the computer?"

"No on a copy disk I made of Josh's data disk for his new project." I heard my father give a muffled exclamation, and rushed on. "I remembered what you and Mom had said, about verifying hypotheses, and giving people the benefit of the doubt. So before I said anything to you, I went to ask Josh about it."

"You *what*?"

"Don't worry, I didn't really tell him anything about Project Aardvark. I swear he had no idea why I was asking. *Aardvark*, Dad; the name showed up again. Josh was angry at my copying his disk. He swears he has no idea what aardvark means, and I believe him. But Dad, there's something fishy. He says he never saw the earlier material. But I saw his eyes when he looked at it, and I'm sure he did."

"How does he explain having the data?"

"Says it only reached him this morning via modem."

"Thor only worked that material out last night," Dad said softly.

The implication hung in the air. "Anyway," I said at last, "Josh's mother came in and invited me to dinner, so I stayed, And I told Josh he'd have to open up more about his work, if we were to — go on. He didn't."

My voice cracked. Dad diplomatically ignored that. "Tell me about those code numbers you sent me the message about," he requested, so I did. All of it. I told him about the other things as well — the snake in the classroom, the encounter with the custodian in the park, and Josh's rescuing me.

"Josh thinks maybe there's a plot to keep me away from the work I'm doing," I finished up. I wanted very much to hear my father laugh at that. He didn't laugh. He started the car motor and drove back home.

The house was quiet as we approached. Mother was sitting at the kitchen table. "Everyone's gone. Thor drove the Quinns home; we can return Mike's car tomorrow. Thor said to tell you he can guess why you two went off, and to call him if you need him and not worry about waking him up. Monahan said you could call him, too. And Sidney has a visitor upstairs."

I went very still. Then I was racing for the stairs, only vaguely conscious that Dad was behind me. I knew what I would see before I saw it — Josh in the office room doorway, silhouetted against the light. Josh haggard, his eyes red-rimmed, but *there*.

"This time I didn't need Samantha to send me," Josh said simply.

Chapter 16

Josh, having faced the fact he had to put his cards on the table, was prepared to do so handsomely. He opened his attaché case and spread its entire contents across my walnut table. He selected a few printouts and pushed them across to Dad and me. "These are the ones you'll be most interested in. They have to do with something known as Aardvark. You're both involved in that in some way, aren't you?"

"You're a very astute young man," Dad murmured.

Josh shook his head. "Not soon enough, where people are concerned. But when Mrs. Webster called my house and was so frantic because Sidney was out alone, I realized something very serious was involved. I'd already decided to come over," he added quickly, catching my reaction. "And I'd already decided Sidney might be in danger. Here's my whole dossier on the work I've been doing in which the name Aardvark's been showing up. Sidney was right; I did see a mention of it earlier in Samantha's memory. When it turned up again, I assumed it was some kind of code. There'd been no mention of the name in my communications with the scientist in California. Yesterday, when Sidney mentioned SACAM —"

My father shot me a look, which I avoided. He did not pursue the matter. He asked Josh, "How did you get this particular commission?"

"The guy contacted me through the box number I listed in a computer newsletter. He said someone else I'd done work for had recommended me. I don't know who. I was to correlate data on an experiment in progress, data which would come to me via a modem hookup between his computer and mine. He also wanted me to perform experiments on a particular computer located in Lakeland. I sent him the work I do over the modem. The telephone number he gave me to use isn't listed, and it's one of those that can communicate only via computers."

Dad and I exchanged glances. "The man knew the Gemini was being tested here?"

"He must have. He asked me to move here and invent a way to get to use it." Josh smiled without humor. "He didn't know I could do that by the easiest way of all — just enroll in the high school as a student."

I stared at him. "You and your mother moved here just so you could do this stealing with Samantha?"

"I didn't know it was stealing! And I

wanted to come here to take courses at the university, anyway. My mother was willing."

Things were going too fast for me. Dad narrowed his eyes. "Let me get this straight. You've had no direct contact with the scientist at all. Just one computer talking to another. All the materials come over untraceable telephone lines between here and California."

"There's nothing so strange about that kind of thing anymore."

"Nothing," Dad said deliberately, "except that this particular material originated here in Lakeland. It still is being researched here, and only here."

For once Josh's impassivity failed him. "*All* of it? You mean this" — he indicated the crowded table — "is the work Sidney's doing?"

"I won't know if it's all that until I've thoroughly checked your printouts. What exactly is your California scientist's research supposed to prove?"

"Basically, that a computer can be operated by *thinking* the entries into it. And that the machine can reply in the same manner, by transmitting its own telepathy." Josh looked scornful. "It sounded like the brainstorm of some crackpot genius, but he's got money behind him, whoever he is. Sent me a retainer in four figures by certified bank check on which his name did not appear. For that, I'm willing to waste time working on his far-out data, especially since he's paying double to have the job done fast. Or as fast as he could get the data to me. It comes in spurts. I figured he was having trouble getting some of his own lab work done."

"Tried out the mental telepathy on the Gemini?" Dad asked casually.

"I know enough about the insides of computers not to waste what little time we have on that." Josh looked at my face, and his eyes widened. "You don't mean you've done it!"

I glanced at my father and saw him give me a faint nod. "A few times," I said quietly. "Not enough to have any real control of it yet, but it *does* work."

Josh regarded me gravely for several minutes. "Just what *is* Project Aardvark?" he asked at last.

It was Dad who answered. "Exactly what you've just described. Operation of a computer by brain waves while the operator's in an alpha state of consciousness. Eventually, receiving responses in the same manner. Either from the computer's own operating system and data program, or by using the computer as a transmitter, the way modems and telephone wires are used now. Except that now the messages have to be read. If this project's successful, messages will one day be transmitted directly, one human brain to computer to another human brain. It's a research project I originated to develop the means for the handicapped — perhaps even the comatose — to use computers to communicate."

Josh looked stunned. "All right," he said at last, "somebody's using Samantha to lift data you or your colleagues have been working on here in Lakeland. Somehow it's getting to California and from there back to me. Is there any way I could get into Samantha's operating system? I mean the actual hardware. I might be able to tell how it's being done."

"There might be." Dad crossed to the telephone and dialed. "Monahan? Any way you can bring that toy you've let Sidney play with over here? *Yes*, right now."

"If you're beginning to wonder if your phone's been bugged," Josh said when he'd hung up, "I can check it. I have a gizmo. In fact, I brought it with me. I've been worried about Sidney, and now I'm more worried. That research of yours could be worth a lot of money and power in the wrong hands."

Josh had checked all our telephones and found them clean by the time Monahan and Jorgensen arrived in a half hour, bringing Samantha in assorted cardboard boxes. "No problem getting her," Monahan said. "She's on loan to me, personally, and all the computers in the lab are mine, rented by the Board of Education. Their way of keeping down the budget, and the start of a business for me when I retire. I can move computers in and out of the school with no red tape, but I'd better have this baby back by morning, or people could start asking questions. What do you want to do?"

"See if she's been programmed to pick up material that's being keyboarded elsewhere than in the lab. She's supposed to have — what? A twenty-five-foot electric field, to eliminate need for an umbilical cord from her operating system to the keyboard? Maybe she has more." Josh released screws and lifted off Samantha's white plastic housing.

We waited in silence, Jorgensen and Monahan hovering over Samantha and assisting when allowed. Mother disappeared, returning with a coffee tray. At last Josh straightened. "Here's your eavesdropper." He held out a small, faintly shining chip. "Samantha's been 'reading' another computer here in Lakeland. Probably in the school, but she has a considerably larger electric field than twenty-five feet. Here, I'll show you."

He reassembled the computer, carried it down to the kitchen, and effectively read on it what Mr. Jorgensen keyed into our own computer in my office.

Josh and Samantha came back upstairs amid a heavy silence.

"I've done most of my Aardvark work on the computer in my school office," Mr. Jorgensen said mechanically. "Using the school phone lines, and my phone credit card, to access an outside mainframe. I thought it was safe enough. I've used my own code. Obviously the thief has cracked the code, or at least found out how to use it."

"Somebody's tapped into Dad's files at the hospital and the university, using Dad's name and access number," I contributed. I turned to my father. "I forgot to tell you. I changed your file codes."

"Good," Dad said, not moving.

"What do you want me to do now?" Josh asked. "I can shut the thief down for a time by just not replacing that chip. But he'll find out, and he'll probably have the chip replaced in no time."

Dad and Thor Jorgensen exchanged glances. "Bring in the FBI?" Dad asked unhappily.

"They'll have to be told," Josh agreed. "But I got the idea you didn't want the government in on this until your research is complete. Besides, having a lot of strange faces crawling around the school would scare the thief off."

It gave me a chill to realize how we were all taking for granted the thief was someone we knew around the school.

"I'd like to nail him," Josh said viciously.

"How?" I asked.

"Set a trap." Josh turned to Monahan. "The housing on Samantha is exactly the same size and shape as what's on my Capricorn. Probably to save the company the time and cost of making a custom housing

for a prototype. I'd like to try a switch —
install the hardware of my Capricorn inside
the Gemini case. Just for twenty-four to
forty-eight hours. That would give me the
chance to set up an internal electronic sabotage of my own. Then we'll put Samantha
back in her own housing, at school, and
Sidney and I will set the trap to catch the
thief."

Dad and the others emphatically thought
things had gotten too dangerous for teen-
agers to be involved.

"Oh, no," I interrupted firmly. "You need
us. We're the protective coloring. Obviously
the — spy — doesn't know yet there's anything special about Josh working with Samantha. Maybe he, or she, thinks everything's being transmitted to California and
staying there. If you men start hanging
around Samantha, instead of Josh and me,
it will definitely look queer."

In the end the others had to agree. "Over
the weekend," Monahan said, referring to
the "borrowing" of Samantha's innards.
"That's about as long as anyone would buy
that it's only gremlins preventing the radar
system from tuning into Thor's computer.
Can you do anything in that time?"

"We'll do it," Josh said grimly. "I don't
like the idea of anybody using this kind of
research material for illegal means."

"I'll broadcast that I'm not using my own
computer in the meantime," Jorgensen sug-

gested. "I can take it away from the school
. . . say it's broken down and is being sent
away for repairs."

"Don't make such a good story that nobody
will buy its reappearance a few days later,"
Dad said dryly.

I stifled a yawn. "Time we knocked off,"
Monahan said briskly, glancing at his watch.

But it was another half hour before Josh
had the inner workings of his Capricorn,
hastily fetched, transferred into Samantha's
frame. It was several hours before either of
us got to sleep.

Chapter 17

A top-level strategy conference convened in our kitchen very early the next morning. Its early hour was for the sake of Monahan, who had to get to the high school before homeroom period in order to set up the bogus SMN Gemini. Samantha, now serenely clothed in the shell of Josh's Capricorn, was upstairs in my office, the only participant in Project Aardvark not represented in the kitchen.

Thor Jorgensen was there, wearing jeans and sweater and bloodshot eyes, having informed the school secretary who handled susbstitute teachers that he was not going to get back from his "emergency family trip out of town" before the weekend after all. Josh was there at Mother's insistence, having spent the night. At six-thirty in the morning, Josh's mental powers were already up to near optimum speed, but the rest of him looked bedraggled. He was jacketless, his shirt sleeves were rolled up, and he had removed his tie. He looked considerably more human.

Dad presided over this impressive-looking gathering. "Are we all clear now? Thor and I will spend the day cooking up some false information for him to feed into his computer." He stopped. "Wait a minute. You just told the school you won't be back for a few days. We don't want you seen yet."

"I can go in tomorrow," Thor corrected. "I often go in to work in my office on a Saturday. The custodians are used to seeing me. It will take most of today to work out the fake data anyway. These guys, whoever they are, are smart. We'll have to give them something close enough to truth for them to buy it, or they'll know they've been discovered and will avoid the trap."

"Tomorrow's the basketball tournament," Monahan said heavily. "There will be team people in and out of **the** building all day."

"Just the people who should see Thor at his computer," Dad said austerely. "A computer jock's the most likely person to be involved."

I shivered. "Do you honestly think any of them could be the — the mastermind behind an operation like this?" I did not mean in computer aptitude alone.

Monahan's face performed what for him was a softening. "I don't think one of our students is operating grand theft and possibly treason, no. I don't even think whoever it is is necessarily aware of the nature and uses of the project involved. Rivington here didn't, and that speaks volumes. But could one of our guys be out to make a few bucks passing on somebody's private research project — especially if that somebody is a teacher? You'd better believe it." He turned to Jorgensen. "Everybody thinks the research you're doing is towards your Ph.D., don't they? That's what you told me it was."

"I *am* hoping to get a Ph.D. out of it," Thor said grimly.

"Okay. I'll let the word leak that your 'family emergency' was in aid of some luscious scientific tidbit for your graduate work." Monahan heaved himself out of his chair. "And I'll make up that list of everybody known to have used the Gemini. I'll get it over here between lunchtime and after school ball practice, whichever comes first. I promised Heller I'd attend that and give him some notes. Rotten time for all this to erupt, isn't it, right before the state championship game? So long, chickadees." He clomped off to his car.

Mother served more coffee and passed around a fresh batch of muffins. I cleared my throat. "Are you guys going to work on the Webster family computer in my office?"

"Nope, in *my* office," Dad said promptly, referring to his study. "Thor and I will bring down our computer. You kids will have to make do with Samantha."

Samantha — she sat there so tranquilly, waiting with deceptive mildness. If all computers had personalities of their own — and they do — Samantha was decidedly a very intelligent, very mischievous flirt. "And if you *dare* to tell me, 'Does not compute' to-day — " I muttered under my breath as I booted up.

Josh gave me a friendly glance. "She's doing that to you, too? I thought she was just sour on me."

"She probably adores you. You're a chal-lenge," I answered grimly. "Look, Samantha, today you've simply got to behave. It's too important."

Y O U   F O R G O T   T O   I N S E R T   D A T A   D I S K , Samantha retorted smugly.

I turned to Josh. "*Which* disk drive? We can't start setting the trap till Dad and Mr. Jorgensen get their work done, and that could take hours."

Josh stretched back in the easy chair and folded his arms behind his head. "We don't have to leave the trap-setting totally up to them. Just how dirty a dirty trick are you prepared to get involved with?"

"That depends," I said warily. I looked at Josh's diabolically angelic countenance, and light began to dawn. "I'm beginning to re-member something. You've already played a few tricks with Samantha in the computer lab, and you never got around to undoing them."

Josh grinned. "Wouldn't it be poetic justice if a four-alarm fire alert went off when our pigeon starts tapping into the fake data?

Especially if Samantha contacts the fire department direct? And maybe a break-in report to the police station, too."

"We don't know whether it will work," I pointed out. "And I don't think my father's going to be thrilled about our setting up an operation like that."

"I have no intention of bringing your father or any other authorities into it," Josh said coolly. "This is something *I* have to do. Are you with me, or not?"

I nodded.

"Good. Let's get started." His eyes narrowed. "You're right about the need for a prior test. If we try anything here, will the others hear downstairs?"

I shook my head. "This room was the family room when I was little. Dad had it thoroughly soundproofed. We don't have a buzzer system like the school, but we do have a burglar alarm. The only trouble is, it's wired for the whole house."

"Show me where the fuse box is, and I'll disconnect the hook-up except in here." We tiptoed down to the basement.

Back upstairs, Josh busied himself with the buzzer hookup, the electric wires behind the baseboard, and Samantha. "I've duplicated what I did in school," he said at last. "You can operate that infernal machine easier than I can. *You* program her to ring the buzzer at a certain signal."

I did so. We took the keyboard and its infrared signal power into the bedroom and closed the door. I gave Samantha the command. The alarm response was gratifyingly loud.

"Now we've proved it will work. I knew it would," Josh said flatly. "Now teach Samantha about the police and fire department telephones. I won't be able to wire her to the phone lines till we get her back into the computer lab." When that was finished, he sat back and scratched his head. "What else could she do?"

A slow smile spread across my face. "In all the TV shows about things like this," I said dreamily, "there are usually bombs going off. With lots of smoke. I keep thinking of the smoke bombs Ceegee and Steve used to set off in the boys' room in junior high sch—"

I stopped abruptly.

"You're worried about them being involved, aren't you?" Josh asked. I nodded. "If they are, it would be like Monahan said," he said flatly. "Semi-innocent small fish in something bigger than they know. They'll be better off caught than if they get in any deeper. And a lot safer. And if they *are* part of the big league—" He left the thought unfinished.

"I feel so helpless!" I burst out. "And don't you tell me it's not my responsibility, like my father does. It became my responsibility the minute I found Project Aardvark material in Samantha's innards."

"I wasn't going to say that," Josh said mildly. "There is something we can do. We were idiots not to think of it last night. We're the computer experts, aren't we? More so than Monahan and Jorgensen and your father. I know *I* am, and I have it on very good authority that you are, too."

I stared at him with slowly dawning comprehension. "Samantha?"

"Samantha. She told me you were the most logical person to work with me. Why can't she tell us the most logical person to be stealing secrets through her capabilities?"

"You mean . . . write a data base system for comparing the possible suspects to the data we know about the criminal?"

"Of course. To begin with, it's somebody who has high computer literacy and access to both Samantha and Jorgensen's data bank." Josh, galvanized, began to stride back and forth as I seated myself before Samantha.

It was not difficult to devise a data base. It was actually fun, so long as we were dealing in the abstract and not feeding in the names of suspects. "When this is over, we could go in business as detectives," I murmured, keyboarding rapidly.

"When this is over, I'm going to nail that job with the California firm." Josh stirred restlessly. "Why doesn't your father get the fake data up here? Why doesn't Monahan call?"

"Monahan has to teach classses, as well as make up a list of suspects. And everybody's probably driving him crazy about the state championship game tomorrow. Josh, will you stop pacing? Lie down! You didn't get any more sleep than I did, and you know it."

Josh threw himself down in an easy chair. I wound up my programming and took the sofa. Josh opened one eye.

"Webster?"

"Mmm?"

"Did you really contact Samantha via brain waves, or was that just bull?"

"It was *not* bull! And don't start about it being a scientific impossibility. Brain waves are electrical energy. It's been proved."

"I know that," Josh said placatingly. "I want to know how you did it."

"By going into alpha state," I answered drowsily. "*I'm* not sure. It's only happened a couple of times. The first, almost by accident. It's like the relaxation response thing that doctors use to help patients control hypertension. Thinking the pulse rate down . . . controlled breathing to the count of four. . ."

I saw a queer look come into his eyes. "Do it now," Josh said quietly. "*No*," he added, as I struggled to sit up. "Keep your eyes closed. You're half asleep anyway. It's a good time." He began to repeat, in a low, even voice, "In — two — three — four. Out — two — three — four. . . ."

"Type 'touchstone' into the keyboard," I murmured.

I heard him doing so, then going back to his seat. The room was very still. It was so peaceful here. So removed from the atmosphere of the computer lab, where there had always been that overtone of fear. But fear lurked now, not far outside these walls. As near as next door, possibly. . .

I had a sudden vivid picture of Ceegee, like a benevolent scarecrow put together by an absent–minded inventor in the dark. Ceegee, who was so clever at computing. Who had cracked all sorts of classified data sources. Who was irritated about my spending so much time with Samantha — and with Josh. Who needed money for college. Who at the Pizza Palace had displayed an unexpected and quite frightening irrationality.

As from a great distance, I heard a whirring, then the soft sounds of Josh's unshod feet padding across the floor. "Webster," he said in a tight voice. I opened my eyes.

Samantha's monitor was flickering. "She can't spell too well," Josh said in that same odd voice. "But otherwise she's quite definitely answered you."

We stared at the screen with mounting tension.

C . G . F I T S S U S P E C T P R O - F I L E , Samantha told us flatly.

Chapter 18

The next twenty-four hours passed very strangely, almost in alpha state. I didn't know what Josh was feeling. He talked little; he looked deep in thought.

It took Dad and Thor Jorgensen an interminable time to produce data accurate enough to pass for real, yet inaccurate enough to betray nothing. While they were doing that, Josh went over and over Samantha's internal system, fine tuning it in a way that would have driven Monahan wild. He invaded the kitchen and had esoteric discussions with my mother over the making of a casserole and a pot of soup. Both turned out superb.

Monahan brought over a list of persons having access to and/or interest in Samantha. He had also, from sources unidentified, provided a dossier on most of the people. Reading it, I almost felt the paper scorch my fingers. Josh's eyebrow lifted.

"We're certainly not supposed to be knowing half this stuff. A lot of these people would be awfully sore."

"We could get in trouble. Monahan could get in trouble. I don't like prying into people's privacy," I said vehemently. "I feel like a spy. It's not what we're supposed to be doing as computer experts."

"It's what a lot of people are doing as computer experts. If Monahan got this material, do you suppose they couldn't, also? Especially if they've tapped into SACAM or other government computer storage? Face it, Webster. Like it or not, we're not just computer programmers anymore. We've become detectives."

"You don't have to sound as if you like it," I answered bitterly. Josh just looked at me.

"What has liking it got to do with it? It's a fact. And another fact is that if we don't do this detecting, somebody else is going to go on having free rein at spying. Do you really think your father's is the only work being stolen?"

"I can face facts, too. I just refuse to be enthusiastic about them," I said irritably.

Actually, we were both having an attack of guilt. For me, this had started out being an exciting game. Oh, I'd been genuinely and deeply worried about the Project Aardvark theft. But I'd also been proud of Dad's bringing me in on it. And intoxicated at the vision of myself as Superwoman. Josh had been on an ego trip, too, and he was also angry at having been used as an unwitting accomplice by the crook.

And last night, when all hell started breaking loose, we'd been something else as well. We had been on a high. But fantasyland ended when you looked at a printout of potential suspects who were classmates and teachers. When you found out things like who had drug or alcohol problems in the family, and who was having trouble paying bills.

We fed Monahan's data into the analysis program we'd written. Samantha rewarded us with a sizable field of names. At least Ceegee wasn't the only prime candidate anymore.

"*You* don't have to be so proud of yourself, either," Josh told Samantha bitterly. His feeling that way made me feel a little better.

Presently Dad and Thor Jorgensen joined us for a conference. Josh inspected what they had produced.

"If you give them this much, they'll suspect something. I usually get chunks of data sent to me at a time, not a whole paper's worth."

Thor grimaced. "That's because I crank the stuff out slowly, and quit when I get stuck. You're right, of course." He reached for a red pencil and started slashing.

It was late afternoon before they had produced something that they all approved. Thor then put it away carefully. "I'll key this in in my school office tomorrow afternoon. And Josh just reminded me of something. You kids mustn't work on this at all first. Computer work's like a fingerprint; it shows the individual operator's own style. Whoever's been using the Gemini would probably recognize the difference."

We assessed strategy. I demonstrated how Samantha could call the police station. I omitted mention of the other, less authority-approved, skills she had learned.

"Okay. I have the number of the area FBI contact, so you can put that in her, too. I've talked to SACAM and the FBI," Thor said. "Not about Project Aardvark, just about a megabucks computer theft in operations. That's breaking enough federal laws, right there. No one's supposed to be using the SACAM network without being government registered and approved. The FBI agreed to hold off closing in here till we've tried out the trap, but they're checking the California phone number Rivington supplied."

Dad straightened. "Then everything's ready. We can get this show on the road as soon as the Gemini system is returned to the school computer lab. There's no reason for Thor to wait till tomorrow to start transmitting."

"No." I didn't even know I'd spoken aloud until I saw everyone looking at me in astonishment. "*No*," I repeated more strongly. "Samantha can't be returned right now; there will still be kids prowling around the school corridors. And tonight it's — risky. If Josh is seen fooling with Samantha, he'll arouse suspicion. He'll have no excuse for being there. The same goes for any of the rest of you who try to keep watch. If Mr. Jorgensen transmits the fake data before Samantha's back in operation, everything gets blown. If he sends it afterwards, tonight they may not know he's filed anything new. But tomorrow night's different."

Dad and Josh looked blank, but Thor grasped the point immediately. "The state championship game. The gym area of the school will be crawling with people. The classroom corridors will all be locked off with those folding metal gates, so anyone who goes into them will either have a key and a good reason, or will have broken in. No accidental passersby and no reason for anyone to find it strange if all of us are on the premises. Half the town will be! And by the time the game starts, the rumor will have spread that I'm back in town and have been working in the office."

"And Sidney and I," Josh said with irony, "will be in the computer lab for the hour before the game begins, with special permission from Monahan to work there on a class project."

He glanced at me, and I saw a grim twinkle in his eye. He was undoubtedly thinking about the smoke bombs.

These matters decided, the meeting dissolved into dinner around the kitchen table, where the Rivington-Webster culinary creations were highly thought of. Mrs. Rivington joined us, on her library supper break, and afterwards Thor drove her back to the library and Josh back home. Monahan, who had declined a dinner invitation on the grounds that two computer-addict faculty members on the premises could arouse suspicion if the place was watched, was brought up-to-date by telephone.

All this left Josh and me with too much to worry over during the remainder of the night. "I've got to stop thinking about it," I told myself doggedly, and on Saturday morning tried to distract my mind by working on Mother's recipes and practicing alpha communication with Samantha.

CONFLICTING SIGNALS, Samantha told me sternly.

"Sidney!" Mother called up the stairs. "Someone's here to see you!"

It must be Josh. Or Cordelia, come to arrange our going together to the game that night. I would have to think of a good excuse that Cordelia would neither suspect nor overrule.

I hurried down the stairs to find Ceegee lounging against a kitchen counter, a mug of coffee in his hand.

"Your ma took pity on me after the long, cold walk I had to get here," he said, gesturing largely.

"Your house migrated across town overnight, I suppose," I responded automatically. Ceegee glanced at Mrs. Webster.

"Smart kid you've raised. I should've cut her down to size when she first mouthed off at me years ago. Get your coat, kid. We're going to take a walk."

"Why should I?"

"Because Coach ordered me to get fresh air and exercise before the big game. You're not going to condemn me to all that ozone alone, are you?" Ceegee's words had the same brotherly teasing tone they always used to, but his eyes looked anxious. I slipped on my coat and boots.

"What's up?" I demanded when we had walked the length of the driveway.

"That's what I wanted to ask you. What the heck was going on last night? First your father's on the phone, asking were you at the house, and when was the last time we'd seen you. Five minutes later he was at the door, to get Steve and me to go out and hunt for you."

I achieved what I hoped was a light, tolerant tone. "I guess Dad just got an attack of Heavy Fatherhood."

"Bull. Your father doesn't get in a flap over nothing, any more than you do." Ceegee turned to face me. "Look, Sid, I got the message about you and me and Rivington. I don't like it, but I won't make a big deal about it or embarrass you again. But this is different. You aren't being you anymore, and that means something's wrong."

I tried to interrupt, but he overrode me. "Sidney, are you in some kind of trouble? Because if you are —"

"Not trouble. I've got — kind of a problem, but I can't talk about it."

"You don't have to talk. But if you need to be bailed out, or rescued, or anything. . . I just wanted you to know the old SOS deal still stands. We're blood brothers, remember?" Ceegee said gruffly. "Okay, that's all I wanted to tell you. See you." He slogged away, a tall ambulatory scarecrow, as I stood looking after him, my eyes filling.

Blood brothers. At eight we had pricked our fingers and mingled drops of blood and sworn an eternal oath. At nine we had used our fathers' CBs — and when I could get my hands on it, Dad's beeper — to signal each other in Morse code when for real or pretend we needed rescuing from unwanted tasks, from uncompleted homework, from parental retribution. And tonight, I might have to betray that oath and turn him in for far more serious offenses, far worse retribution. I turned slowly back towards home, wishing the issue were as clear cut as Josh made it seem.

Dad spent most of Saturday at the hospital, observing as much as possible his usual routine. Among other things, he keyed false data into his data file in the hospital's mainframe system, just in case it too had been invaded. He came home at four to report that Thor was now installed in the school science office, keyboarding away. He would not be finished until six, which was when the basketball fanatics would be arriving to stake out choice seats in the bleachers. The teams and related staff would be checking in. Thor would stroll down to the locker room to wish everyone well and bear witness to his own return.

At six o'clock Josh and I, armed with a pass signed by Monahan, would be let in (by Monahan) to the computer lab. Monahan would have hung one of his famous "Now Hear This" notices on the inside of the door, as if by accident covering its one clear glass pane. We were being driven by my mother, with Samantha's operating system in cartons in the car. Monahan, of course, had already returned the fake Gemini to the lab.

I had some trouble convincing my parents to let me be in on this little shindig. "Josh needs a witness," I pointed out firmly. "It will be safer if two of us are there. We're lab partners, so it will look natural. And if there's any danger, Samantha will protect us!"

"I know. Those alarm triggers you rigged up. I just hope the gremlins don't short-circuit them," Dad said. He did not look happy.

We rode the six blocks to the school in silence. Lights poured from school windows, and the floodlights in the parking lot rimmed the rooftops, causing their sheets of ice to sparkle. There was another cold, distant sparkle to the moon.

Josh glanced at it briefly. "We can put men

on the moon, but we can't get humans to treat each other decently here on earth."

"At least we're preventing something indecent." My voice cracked slightly.

Josh picked up two of Samantha's cartons and we started toward the school. The side door was open, with Monahan inside it. "Hurry up. I've got to get back to the gym in five minutes, so get moving." His face looked like the wartime photographs of Winston Churchill.

No one was in the school corridor as we went down it. Monahan unlocked the folding gate, opened it just far enough for us to slip through, and locked it behind us. He unlocked the computer lab. "I left the lights on when I came in earlier. Don't lose your passes, and bolt the door again after me."

We didn't have to be told that.

Monahan left. Josh locked up behind him. I was already unpacking Samantha's innards. Josh ignored them and brought out his electronic detection device. "What on earth are you doing?" I asked, startled.

"What does it look like I'm doing?" Josh clapped his hand over my mouth as I started to speak. Then he grabbed paper and pencil from Monahan's desk and scribbled quickly. *Front office has 2-way intercom. Anyone could be listening in.*

I nodded swiftly. I said aloud in my usual angry-with-Josh voice, "Do we *have* to work on this stuff tonight? When I hired on with you, I had no intention of missing the championship game."

"We just have to get the extra stuff done for that hardware company. You'll be out of here by the time the game starts, or soon after," Josh answered with authority. As he spoke, his hands moved swiftly over the bookshelves, the baseboards, the desks. Over the doorframes, and the picture of George Washington hanging on the wall. Over the blackboards, over the telephone. Over the window frames. He fingered an okay sign to me and started unscrewing Samantha's own housing from the fake Gemini machine.

I positioned myself against the door, blocking his activities even more from sight. "What does this man mean, he wants a FIFO and not LIFO inventory system?" I inquired.

We went through an entire dialogue about the inventory system of a hardware manufacturer while Josh put Samantha back together.

"Okay, I'm going home," Josh said loudly when he'd finished. "You staying for the game?"

"Of course!"

"Suit yourself." As he spoke, he was booting up Samantha. My eyes asked a question, and Josh's lips formed the answer without making sound. *Keying in to the intercom to check the halls.* We listened in to all the other areas of the school. The gym was a madhouse. The game had started. A student announcer hailed plays by Steve, by Ceegee. *So they're right where they ought to be*, I thought, relieved.

There was no noise at all in the locker room. Heller Hazzard could be heard in the gym office, explaining to a second-string player why he'd been benched for failing grades.

There was no noise, not even the sound of footfall, in the corridors leading to the computer lab.

Josh looked at me and nodded. I went to the door, unbolted it, opened and slammed it, and bolted it again, as Josh closed down Samantha. He took a swift look around to make sure we'd left no trace, before I snapped out the lights. By feel and instinct, with me leading, we made our way to Monahan's office and closed ourselves inside.

We dared not risk a light, and we dared not risk the creak of furniture. We settled for, and on, the floor. Remaining here was one of the plans we had not shared with our elders. Dad and Thor Jorgensen knew only that Samantha would send off signals as soon as someone keyed her in to the computer in Thor's office. They did not know my determination to first capture some damaging evidence of Project Aardvark's theft, or of Josh's determination to be in at the kill.

My right leg started aching under me. Josh flexed his fingers. I remembered something suddenly and caught my breath. Then

I leaned close to Josh's ear and whispered, "Stink bomb?" He put my hand to his chin so I could feel him nod his head.

We waited.

In the dead stillness we caught a faint whirring sound. The intercom. Someone was using the office intercom to check this room, then turned it off again. The hairs on the back of my neck began to rise.

Another interminable wait.

Then there were footsteps. Then there were closer footsteps. They stopped outside the classroom door, but not from apprehension. Whoever stood there was just getting out a key. There was a faint click, then the dead bolt turned.

The door opened. The door closed again. The bolt slipped to. Then footsteps, soft, almost unhearable . . . *rubber soles*.

We heard the faint, unmistakable whirr of Samantha booting up.

No light had gone on. Josh, cautiously, eased himself to his feet; peered through the glass of Monahan's office door. I followed. A tensor lamp had been set up and turned on at Samantha's station. It shone downward, at her keyboard, so all we could see was that narrow stream of light. Samantha's housing hid the keyboard and the hacker's hands. As we watched, the tensor was snapped off.

Despite myself, I felt a swift sharp stab of admiration. This hacker was *good*, good enough to work in the dark, with nothing visible but the symbols on Samantha's screen.

We waited till we felt sure the hacker had had long enough to capture some of the fake Aardvark data on the monitor, then Josh slid like a panther through the office doorway. The door as he opened it had made no sound. I slipped my feet out of my shoes and followed.

Josh went unerringly down the side aisle, so he could overtake the hacker from behind. I positioned myself next to the classroom door. As soon as I counted to ten, I would snap on the lights. Josh, counting also, had his hands poised to come down on the hacker's shoulders, jerking him backwards before he could black out the computer screen.

Light flooded the room. Josh's hands closed around the startled, unprepared shoulders of the gym teacher, Heller Hazzard.

Chapter 19

For a split second, all three of us were motionless. Heller recovered first.

"What the devil do you kids think you're doing, breaking into a school classroom at night?" His voice had exactly the right note of amusement and reproof, and I answered automatically.

"We have a pass."

It was possible for Hazzard to be in there for perfectly legitimate reasons, but in that case he would not be accepting Josh's grasp. In that case the fake data would not be showing on the screen.

"You're breaking into a classified data bank, and we know it." Josh tightened his grasp on Hazzard's arms as the teacher tried to move. I took one step away from the door and my voice came out like a child's, shocked and disbelieving.

"It was you. *You've* been stealing my father's alpha research and selling it . . . to whom?"

We were not prepared for Hazzard to break as quickly as he did. The resistance drained from his body; his head dropped on his hands. "I don't know who. I don't know what all this is about. I'm an athlete — I *was* an athlete — not a scientist. I needed the money, and a guy called and offered me this job —"

Like an instant retrieve, the data on Hazzard's extravagant, demanding wife flashed into my mind. I stared at Josh, torn. Josh's eyes were just as compassionate, but he spoke gruffly. "We can't let it go. There's too much involved."

"Nobody's asking you to let it go," Hazzard answered, just as gruffly. "You can take the whole damn data disk to the police." He sounded as if we'd awakened him from a nightmare. "I'm off the hook now. *I* didn't put you onto this. I couldn't help it, so I've nothing to lose —"

On the contrary, you have a great deal to lose.

Neither of us had seen or heard anyone approach. But suddenly, the door had opened up behind me. I swung round, got only one stunned glimpse before an iron arm locked around me and the cold metal of a pistol was pressed against my head.

It was Wiggins, the custodian. Even his speech now was different; it was well-educated, crisp. My frantic gaze fell on Hazzard. He too was stunned — not by the transformation, but by the custodian's presence and involvement.

Mr. Anonymous in California had planted a spy here to keep an eye on Heller. Heller hadn't known that.

"You didn't think you would be trusted on your own on a matter of this importance, did you?" The voice near my ear asked Hazzard with contempt. "You don't have the stomach or the courage. That was evident in your athletic career. Now you let go of him and step back, young man, and don't make a move toward that computer or the young lady here will pay for it."

They must still want something from Heller — what? Of course — the latest data on Project Aardvark. They needed Heller for it, which proved the "custodian" was a goon and not a hacker.

Only, when Heller had retrieved all the forged data, then what? The fake had not been designed as a wrap-up of the experiment. It would come to a dead stop, midstream, so to speak, quite shortly. The California connection might — probably did — have enough on Heller Hazzard to keep him tractable for future use. It had nothing to hold over Josh and me.

As the implication in this sank in on us, Josh backed off, hands up, saying in his most placating voice, "Okay, okay!"

He was three feet from Hazzard now, four feet from Samantha. Too far away to key in the alarms. Too far from Wiggins to disable him if the buzzer system went off first, as it was programmed to do after ten minutes of uninterrupted keyboarding.

"Get to work," Wiggins ordered Hazzard. The gun moved slightly, painfully along my cheek.

I felt Josh's eyes boring into me. Josh said, deliberately, "What we need is a touchstone."

Touchstone.

I had less than ten minutes. I closed my eyes and tried not to think about impossibilities. *Breathe slowly . . . four in, four out. . . . See something tranquil. . . .* From my unconscious I summoned a memory of the lake on an autumn day, its wedding ring of glowing trees reflected in the quiet waters, the white swans floating. I felt my limbs relax, felt myself seem to float lazily upward. T O U C H-S T O N E . . . T O U C H S T O N E . . . S A M A N T H A , R E A D M E. D O N O T S H O W R E S P O N S E. R E-P E A T : D O N O T S H O W R E-S P O N S E.

A prickle ran down my spine. Words blazed across a screen behind my eyes. M E S S A G E R E C E I V E D. G I V E C O M M A N D.

I went limp in Wiggins' arm, and focused my concentration with a fierce intensity. S T I N K B O M B . . . S T I N K B O M B. I could only pray Josh had not given Samantha that command in some weird code. I mustn't think about that. I must hold myself ready, and keep thinking stink bomb.

There was a clap like a car backfiring, and suddenly the room was filled with noxious smoke. I sensed, rather than saw, Josh diving through its cover. Hazzard jerked back from the work station and was coughing hard.

I heard Wiggins coughing. The gun was still against my ear. Don't think about that — *no*, think about it, *use* it . . . see the way you used to play with the CB. I willed the message to Samantha. D E L T A . . . D E L T A . . . A L L A L A R M S. And then, swiftly, in the Morse code Ceegee and I used to use so long ago, S O S . . . R O O M T W O T E N . . . S O S . . . .

The alarms exploded into life. The buzzers sounded. In the split second when I felt the grip on me weaken, I jerked myself away. Just in time — Josh straightened, and his leg shot out, catching Wiggins with a swift karate stroke which was rapidly followed by another.

It was all over when, two minutes later, Ceegee charged in breathing fire, followed by Monahan and other members of the newly named state champion basketball team.

Chapter 20

The basketball team's planned celebration at the Pizza Palace took place in the Websters' kitchen instead. It took place, actually, all through the house, for the crowd was considerable. Interviewing by police and FBI was going on upstairs in my office. All parties involved with the tournament game and/or Project Aardvark were somewhere in the house, with two conspicuous exceptions. Heller Hazzard was in the Lakeland police station, awaiting the arrival of his lawyer. Wiggins, his true identity still unknown, had been removed to the Hackensack County jail where he was being very closely watched.

Newspaper reporters, and the TV crews that had been at the school to cover the championship game were kept downstairs by Mom, where they gathered material on the basketball team, not to mention Monahan's computer classes, while waiting for an official statement to be released.

Release, I thought as I hurried around,

shaking off questions, *is the operative word*. I was released from my captor, thanks to Josh and Samantha. Project Aardvark was released from the threat — no, the reality — of being stolen, for whatever purpose. I was more and more sure, from how the FBI authorities were acting, that the purpose had been decidedly bad.

Heller Hazzard, I suspected, regarded his arrest as almost a release — in more ways than one. Monahan, before coming over, stopped by the Hazzard house to break the news. Mrs. Hazzard's concern was all for herself and how Heller had failed her; what a fool he was.

"She thought she was marrying a big baseball star. How could she be expected to settle for a nobody teacher?" Josh said caustically when he heard this.

The FBI man who was listening to all this smiled. "The two teachers here haven't been exactly nobodies," he said appreciatively. Monahan just looked impassive, Thor rather embarrassed, and Dad grinned.

"Oh, the drudgery of being merely a hospital chief of staff! I had to sit out the whole affair." He contemplated me and added pointedly, "Of course, I was not aware the evening was going to turn into a Fourth of July spectacular."

I stirred uncomfortably. Josh just raised an eyebrow. "Necessary secrecy. If you'd known what we'd had in mind, you'd have said no. We might still have caught Hazzard, but not that other goon."

"Of course I'd have said no. It was far too dangerous. All the same, I can't help admiring your enterprise. Not to mention creativity." Dad stroked his beard meditatively. "Stink bombs, yet. I haven't set one of those in thirty years."

Josh and I looked at each other. It was time we disentangled ourselves and let Dad, Monahan, and Jorgensen handle such touchy subjects as Josh's wiring Samantha into the police phone line, and my checking certain matters out in certain highly forbidden data banks.

"If you gentlemen are finished with us, we have some friends waiting downstairs. You know how to find us if we're needed." Josh rose and bowed formally, the effect somewhat marred by the fact he wasn't wearing his Chief Executive Officer clothes. He was in jeans and sneakers, an outfit I hadn't known he owned. He was in them, I felt sure, only because he'd correctly anticipated a need for silent footwork and karate, but the end result was that he looked deceptively like just another kid. This disarmed the authorities, and would certainly make Josh more acceptable to the crowd downstairs.

As it turned out, I need not have worried about *that*. Our evening's exploits had established him as an okay eccentric. One reporter was already referring to us as computer detectives, and I had a sneaking suspicion that the phrase would stick. The computer jocks, meanwhile, were developing a sudden interest in the marital arts.

"One more obsession. That's all they need!" Cordelia groaned. I chuckled.

"You'll survive. Or we could study judo or tai quan doh along with them. After tonight I'm beginning to think I should."

"After tonight I think anybody will think twice before messing around with you," Cordelia laughed.

It was two a.m. before Josh and I had our first chance to speak privately together. By then everyone else had finally gone home.

Josh followed me up to the office, yawning.

I eyed him. "You should go home and sleep for forty-eight hours."

"I think I can — now." Josh threw himself down in the big chair, hoisted his feet to the ottoman, and sprawled. "You don't look tired at all," he decided, contemplating me through one open eye.

"I'm not. I feel like I'm on a high. Maybe it's too much alpha state. Maybe I'm not slap happy." I curled upon the sofa, looked at his decidedly undignified posture, and could not suppress a giggle. "This is getting to be a habit with us."

"We've got to stop meeting like this," Josh murmured. Coming from him, that was tantamount to a stand-up monologue from Johnny Carson. "I haven't had a chance to tell you," he continued, "my mother brought over a telegram that arrived at the apartment while I was out. That guy from California's flying in tomorrow for some kind of trade show or convention."

"Oh?"

"He and some of his top execs. He wants me to meet him in the city to discuss that job he offered me."

I relaxed. "I thought you meant the Project Aardvark thief."

"Didn't you hear? The FBI arrested *him* as soon as our local boys notified them that we'd closed down the operation here." Josh got back to what now concerned him more. "I'll go in and see the men, and see what kind of money they have in mind. I wouldn't take the job till school gets out, of course, so I'll have work for you till then, if you want it. I'll try to get you free-lance assignments, once I'm in California. Interested?"

"I might be."

It would be a lot more peaceful, working without Josh. A lot less stressful, a lot less argumentative. Suddenly, none of those virtues seemed particularly appealing.

Josh yawned again and hauled himself to his feet. "I'd better go if I want to be in shape to talk business tomorrow afternoon. Those forty-eight hours will have to wait till afterwards. Maybe — maybe till after we celebrate my new job."

It sounded remarkably as if he was trying to ask me for a date. It also sounded as if he didn't know how. I accompanied him downstairs to the door. Only a glow from the outside light, and the banked embers in the fireplaces, broke the dimness. I opened the door and Josh stood there, irresolute.

He wanted to kiss me, but he clearly didn't know how to go about it. Instead he blurted, "Good night," and took off in a rush.

It was early evening before he showed up on our doorstep the next day. I took one look at his face and exclaimed, "What happened?"

"Can I have a cup of coffee first? I just got off the bus from New York, and I need it." Josh plunged for the stairs without bothering to greet my parents.

I took the tray of coffee things up to the office and shut the door behind me firmly. "What happened? Didn't you take the job?"

"What do *you* think?" Josh asked bitterly. "Only you used the wrong verb. I didn't *get* the job. They'd seen us on TV this morning, and they'd already made up their minds I was too young! Practically patted me on the head, and told me to come back and see them in ten years."

He took the coffee mug and threw himself into his usual chair. "You said you were on a high last night. I must have been on one, too, deluding myself. These shortsighted reactionary bureaucrats aren't interested in ability and drive, only in who fits the mold. Not too young, not too old."

"They don't sound like people you'd want

to work with, anyway," I said diplomatically. Josh flashed me a wry glance.

"You're right. But that doesn't get around the fact that my career's been set back a decade. Nobody's going to hire someone with a thirty-five-year-old brain, when he's chronologically an adolescent and looks like a kid!"

That was when the brainstorm struck me with the blinding clarity of Samantha responding to me via alpha waves. I saw the whole thing, perfect and complete.

I took a deep breath. "*I'd* hire you," I said sweetly. "Sidney Scott Webster, President; SSW ENTERPRISE, *computer consultants.*" Dad was right, I did have a good name for an executive.

"Maybe SSW Incorporated." Yes, that would be good. "Nobody's going to be concerned about our ages if they're hiring a *company*, not employees."

I had him hooked, though of course he wasn't ready to admit it. "Why don't *I* incorporate," he demanded, "and you can work for me?"

"No way!"

"Why not?"

"Because, to be blunt, you'd fail. You're a genius, but you're not a good administrator, and I am. You're lousy at time management, and you know it, and you're not exactly brilliant at people management, either. You're great at logic, but your logic takes too long."

"You mean it doesn't take in the human factor," Josh murmured. I could see the wheels going around in his head.

I threw the *coup de grace*. "Besides, I have a major asset. Monahan doesn't want to keep Samantha in the high school any more. He says it's too much responsibility. So Dad and Jorgensen telephoned California, and pulled strings. From now on, Samantha lives with me."

A slow smile spread across Josh's face. "It's an idea," he admitted. "It's definitely an idea. To tell the truth, it would be a relief not to have to deal with administrative garbage. But who's going to go out and sell the services of the computer detectives?"

"*I* am. You," I said kindly, "would set clients' teeth on edge."

"You think they're going to take a blue-eyed ingenue any more seriously than they do me?"

He was asking for trouble, and he knew it. He was also stalling for time. "Being a blue-eyed blonde ingenue is an advantage," I said haughtily. "I'm a discriminated against minority. I'm a female. All the big companies right now need some 'token women' to make them look good, and get them off the hook with the government's equal opportunity law. I'd be an idiot not to take advantage of that. They'll fall all over themselves at the chance to get a token woman they think isn't any threat."

"Boy," Josh said, "are they going to get fooled." The look in his eyes made me feel intoxicated again.

"Besides," I added, slightly breathless, "when I put my hair up and wear a suit and heels, I look older than you do." I ducked as he threw a sofa cushion at me.

The cushion missed, but Josh did not. He dove across to pin me against the wall. "If you want to get loose," he threatened, "you'd better apologize for that snide crack!"

But he was laughing. I was laughing, too. All at once, we weren't laughing anymore. All at once, he was feeling like kissing me, again. Only this time he did. And he knew exactly how.